BARET MAGARIAN was
Armenian origin. He was educat
universities and has published *... ... ...... (Pleasure
Boat Studio), *Mirror and Silhouette* (Albion Beatnik Press),
and *Chattering with All my Favourite Beasts* (Ensemble).
He has worked as a lecturer, translator, musician, journalist,
nude model, stage director, and book representative.

*Also by Baret Magarian*

*The Fabrications* (Pleasure Boat Studio)
*Melting Point* (Italian; Quarup)
*Mirror and Silhouette* (Albion Beatnik Press)
*Chattering with All My Favourite Beasts* (Ensemble)

# MELTING POINT

## BARET MAGARIAN

CROMER

PUBLISHED BY SALT PUBLISHING 2019

2 4 6 8 10 9 7 5 3 1

Copyright © Baret Magarian, 2019

Baret Magarian has asserted his right under the Copyright, Designs and Patents Act 1988 to be identified as the author of this work.

*This book is sold subject to the condition that it shall not, by way of trade or otherwise, be lent, resold, hired out, or otherwise circulated without the publisher's prior consent in any form of binding or cover other than that in which it is published and without a similar condition including this condition being imposed on the subsequent publisher.*

This book is a work of fiction. Any references to historical events, real people or real places are used fictitiously. Other names, characters, places and events are products of the author's imagination, and any resemblance to actual events or places or persons, living or dead, is entirely coincidental.

First published in Great Britain in 2019 by
Salt Publishing Ltd
12 Norwich Road, Cromer, Norfolk NR27 0AX United Kingdom

www.saltpublishing.com

Salt Publishing Limited Reg. No. 5293401

A CIP catalogue record for this book is available from the British Library

ISBN 978 1 78463 197 0 (Paperback edition)
ISBN 978 1 78463 198 7 (Electronic edition)

Typeset in Neacademia by Salt Publishing

Printed and bound in Great Britain by Clays Ltd, Elcograf S.p.A

For my mother.
In the end you transmitted so much light.

# CONTENTS

| | |
|---|---|
| Crime and Bread | 1 |
| The Watery Gowns | 10 |
| Erasing the Waves | 21 |
| Island | 40 |
| The Mosque of Córdoba | 74 |
| Clock | 82 |
| The Chimera | 89 |
| The Rich and the Slaughtered | 97 |
| The Meltdown | 104 |
| The Balls | 113 |
| The Visitation | 127 |
| Alba | 137 |
| The Fever | 155 |
| The Opiate Eyes of the Buddha | 174 |
| | |
| *Acknowledgements* | 212 |
| *Notes* | 213 |

# MELTING POINT

# CRIME AND BREAD

WHEN SHE LOOKED out of the window of the café, as the Astrud Gilberto song finished, it looked like rain. They didn't predict this, she thought, as she pressed the glasses up her nose. They rested for a few minutes, only to succumb to gravity again. A shaft of sunlight pierced the cloudy, filmy lines and something exotic crept up her nostrils, an aroma of something half forgotten. With that guarantee in her pocket, or under her skin, in her nostrils or floating around her brain, she tumbled out onto the street, gladly performing the street walk she'd been rehearsing like a samba. She was ready for her dance with the world, she was shining and beaming, a newly-minted coin. The trees made way for her, passers-by admired her from near and from far. They smiled at her nonchalance, they tried to guess her age, whether or not she had any interesting birthmarks, or was hiding the insignia of childbirth or loss, whether or not she had a husband or boyfriend, whether she was a fiery lover or a passionless one.

Now it's my time, she thought, I've waited long enough, now I'm ready, washed, cleaned, perfumed, my hair is immaculate, my skin is porous and my eyes are pellucid. See if you can catch me!

At a street corner life leapt at her like a newly-released cat, claws exposed. Little children played, cars honked, bankers drew up investment plans, mortgages and loans, mothers worried, fathers fornicated, city dwellers dreamt of the country, artists saved coupons, priests considered Paul's epistles to the Romans.

But life only makes sense to me when I'm burning the candle at both ends, I can't stand that dullness, when things go stale, I can't stand that grey area. I need sequins, raisins, spices from Morocco, French wines. What would they say if they saw me tail-spinning out of control, intravenous needles hanging from me, would I be like that astronaut from 2001 as he enters the star gate, perpetually glazed eyes? I've breakfasted and starved, waited tables, taught kids, life-modelled, sang at auditions, made soufflés, answered the telephone, shepherded tourists. When was I really me? And what would it take to make me lose myself? Maybe if I could get into a really bad accident, get stabbed by a stranger, drink a bottle of brandy neat . . .

*Reine de joie par Victor Joze . . . . chez tous les libraires.* That bit of French caught her attention. She came to a standstill in front of a window pane. Behind the window was another pane of glass surrounded by a wooden frame, underneath it there was a poster. Such wonderful colours: a bronzed, sunset orange that had stepped out of Tunisia, she imagined though she'd never been, the yellowing brown lettering in old-style charm. Grace and squalor were combined as the slightly emaciated woman with a skeletal arm planted a somehow tender kiss on the nose of the old, bald, half sleeping fatty with the bloated belly. The woman looked innocent despite it all, with her neck wrapped in a brown ribbon and her red dress. Perhaps that was what drew her to the poster, that innocence, or was it the single brown curl of hair on the woman's forehead, it was beautiful, distinctive.

Had she ever really looked at a poster or a painting, she wondered? Who was the other man on the woman's left, some

English brigadier, a buffoon, or prude, with his faintly ridiculous orange-red moustache?

※

Later, in the evening, in her flat, outside which vines crept upwards, inside which cat-smells spread, she was in the kitchen mixing spaghetti and a sauce she had carelessly prepared. In her hand, on and off, a goblet of red wine. In her mouth, on and off, a rolled-up cigarette. In her eyes, all the time, a far-off look. She was thinking of that Toulouse-Lautrec print and how nice it would look next to her book case, which was not full of books at all, but magazines about furniture, motor bikes, graphics, landscape gardening, tree surgeons, lingerie, package holidays, mountaineering. She had put up a shelf and dismantled a table, painted her sister's living room, driven a Harley Davidson in California, tried to design a webpage, used a Ouija board at a party, planted an apple tree, admired Japanese gardens, dressed in a black négligé for an old boyfriend, avoided package holidays and hated the idea of mountaineering, being afraid of heights.

In her dreams that night she entered the Toulouse-Lautrec poster, or rather, its essence turned into a scenario she became part of.

She was in a café, which she knew in her dream to be Parisian. The clientele was an elegant one, dressed in velvet, capes, and dinner jackets, like the three figures in the painting. She recognised the old, fat, bald man and the red brigadier, but she couldn't find the lady and she had the dim sense that she couldn't find her because *she* was that lady. At the far end of this café, the shape and size of which seemed to fluctuate so that at some moments it appeared vast and at others small, she noticed a long string of flamboyant women – courtesans, she realised. She regarded them from a stool at the bar and sipped a glass of absinthe. As she perused the crowd, she noticed that some of them had assumed very distinctly the appearance of figures from famous paintings: Van Gogh's self-portrait, Munch's screaming skull. On turning her attention to the bar again, she knew that the old fat slob was expecting a kiss from her, the very same kiss she had seen her counterpart in the poster plant on his nose. But she couldn't do it, and she felt his irritation grow. A tall man in a top hat flicked a pair of dandyish black gloves across her hands until she finally had to relent. As she kissed him everything altered. She was aware of the sounds of the ocean. A blue sea ebbed and pulsed with virile life.

When she woke up the next morning, the dream came back to her as she sipped a cup of weak Earl Grey tea. On her way to the dentist's surgery where she worked as a receptionist, she wondered whether she might be able to somehow steal the poster. She could have afforded to buy it, that wasn't the issue, she just felt that stealing it would represent some kind of victory over life, would amount to an act of necessary defiance.

In the evening she was reading, her eyeglasses slowly slipping down her nose.

Maya tells this story:

*A man is on his way to the bakery in search of a loaf of bread. On his way there he comes across a fresh loaf lying on the road, still in its wrapping. For a moment he hesitates. Should he pick up the loaf and so save himself a visit to the bakery? Or should he go through with his original plan? In the end he decides to pick up the loaf of bread. As he bends down, he is run over by a bus. By a miracle the loaf stays undamaged. As an ambulance arrives, a man turns up and, seeing the bread, takes it home and eats it.*

She kept thinking about the story.

She rang a friend, his name was Gilbert, he was extremely myopic and owned a pet snake.

She read him the story and asked, 'What do you think this means?'

Gilbert said that he would have to think about it.

'Well, this is what I think,' she said. 'It might mean: the Man was stealing, in a sense, the loaf of bread that he found on the road, or rather he shouldn't have tried to take what wasn't his, or what he hadn't paid for . . . . and when he did, he was punished by being run over. That ends that. But then someone else comes along and "steals" that same loaf and he gets away with it, which suggests the randomness and imprecision of cosmic crime and punishment . . . plus it could be argued, of course, in this interpretation, that the punishment the first man receives was excessively harsh. Or maybe the Second Man gets away with taking the loaf of bread because he never had the intention of going to the bakery as the First Man had, which leads me to the second interpretation: the First Man betrayed his original impulse, and by so doing, created a new problem for himself. He isn't punished, he merely suffers the consequences of not being true to himself. The Second Man is true to himself and doesn't hesitate or get side-tracked. But does this mean that to commit what might be regarded as an unscrupulous, or rather unfeeling act (after all, the Second Man has presumably just witnessed the First Man being run over by a bus) is all right so long as you don't question yourself or as long as that act is true to the original instinct which it honours? What do you think? Gilbert?'

Gilbert said that he would have to think about it.

After a goblet of red wine, she concluded that she should steal the poster.

She stayed awake until 4 a.m., reading and drinking wine. By then she was so drunk that if someone had pricked her with a sewing needle she would have felt nothing. Her limbs were relaxed and inert and her eyes glazed and bloodshot. She rummaged around for an empty bottle of Glenmorangie, a fairly hefty bottle which she kept for sentimental reasons. She stuffed it inside her overcoat and began to walk to the shop.

She stopped a few feet away from the shop and looked around her. The street was deserted and quiet. The moon seemed to be burning up the sky. Slowly she removed the bottle from her overcoat and crept towards the window. Gripping the bottle tightly she looked at the poster, admiring it more than ever, its finesse, its subtlety. She scrutinised the pane of glass, judging it to be quite flimsy, no match for the bottle of Glenmorangie. The resulting alarm would probably be dismissed by those awaking to its vile whining as a malfunction. She steadied herself, took aim and hurled the bottle, it became a missile. The glass shattered with shocking loudness. A little bit stunned, she scrambled towards the display, avoiding the shards of glass that showered across the pavement. It was only then that she noticed no alarm was sounding. A second later a dog started barking insanely. She grabbed the poster, which was small enough to fit under her sprawling overcoat. She was expecting sleepy people to seep out in droves, she was expecting howling sirens and police cars, she was expecting someone to make a citizen's arrest. But nothing, no one. She was back at her flat in a matter of minutes and on her way there she encountered no one.

It was done.

The next morning, in her sobriety, she expected her doorbell to ring, but it didn't. She expected someone to stop her on the way to work, but they didn't. The world had hardly even batted an eyelid.

When she got home from the surgery, she breathed a sigh of relief and stared at the poster. She couldn't quite believe that she had done it.

A week passed and she summoned up the courage to walk past the shop. There was a new pane of glass there, thicker. In the place of the Toulouse-Lautrec now there was a virile seascape by Emile Goüter.

But now, rather than giving her pleasure, each time she looked at the poster, she felt pangs of guilt. The release, or health, or energy, she had hoped for didn't come and she thought about confessing her crime to the shop owner, but decided against it. Eventually she wrapped it up, shoved it in a parcel, and mailed it back to the shop with an anonymous apology.

She was reading an article about Japanese gardens, vegetable moussaka was cooking in the oven, and her goblet of red wine stood on a little table. She was back to normal, she had practically forgotten the whole thing. Then the phone rang. It was Gilbert.

'I was thinking about that story, do you remember . . . ?'

After a puzzled moment she did.

'How did it go, like this, right . . . the First Man wants the loaf, sees one on the street, gets run over, the Second Man sees it and takes it and eats it, right?'

'Yeah, I think that's it.'

'Well, I was wondering: how did that loaf get into the middle of the road in the first place?'

'The story doesn't say.'

'But it's obvious, someone must have stolen that loaf, then they had second thoughts and decided to abandon it.'

'But why in the middle of the road? Why not in a dustbin?'

'They probably thought it would be too wasteful, so they wanted to give someone, a tramp perhaps, or someone on the breadline – if you will excuse the pun – someone very poor, the opportunity to claim it without knowing it was stolen.'

'This is all very speculative,' she insisted.

'Of course. Well, what's your explanation for how the loaf got there?'

'Someone dropped it by accident.'

'Then why didn't they pick it up?'

'They didn't want a dirty loaf of bread.'

'But it was still in its wrapping.'

'Ok, you win, Gilbert.'

'Or maybe the Second Man who comes along and picks it up had dropped it earlier, before the story begins. And he was just coming back to claim what was rightfully his?'

She said she would have to think about it.

*Crime and Bread*

Eventually she went back to the shop and was greatly relieved to see the poster in its frame back in its original spot in the window. Without a moment's hesitation she decided to buy it and even insisted on paying a little bit more, to the assistant's astonishment. He responded to her generosity by taking special care when wrapping it up, tying it in a single brown curling ribbon. Once she was the rightful and legal owner, clutching it proudly, the fog in her brain lifted and life took on a new clarity. As she walked she felt the first intimations of spring. She stopped in the middle of a quiet street, where hardly any cars passed. Looking around furtively as though she was about to carry out another crime, she laid the poster down gently in the middle of the road. Then she walked home.

# THE WATERY GOWNS

I

IN THE SEA, ever changing, ever redefining its shape, the divers felt life pulsing through them as they plunged downwards into that vast world where every kind of life and colour and light existed. That underwater universe was as rich and variegated as the one above. In three they went and they had no need of words, just gestures and signals that they all instinctively understood. Everything down there was disembodied, slow moving, the divers were shadowy, stripped of their faces, hidden behind masks, their skin hidden behind diving suits, their mouths concealed by their breathing apparatus, oxygen cylinders turning their backs bumpy and rounded. The odd refraction of light; soundwaves quelled by the cushioning glory of water and unimpeded space. Shoals of fish darted this way and that, undisturbed by the three divers, who watched them in fascination. Every now and then a weirdly shaped fish, a tapered apparition rolled and passed by and then twos and threes followed, perfect replicas of one another, clones, recurring moments; their gauzy, distorted forms made the divers think the sea contained more mysteries than any earthly realm. The truths and feelings to be found down there could not be communicated to anyone who had not experienced that dark, luminous abyss, that underwater garden.

One of the divers pointed to a distended shell, half-hidden by a faintly glowing shrub. The shrub seemed to be coated in a phosphorescent substance and the tallest of the trio extracted the shell, which resembled a human ear stretched into weird plasticity. It sank from end to end like an overburdened rope bridge. The shell was promptly set down in an underwater case where it took its place with a hundred others like it and yet different. Later those shells, small, large, odd, intricate, gaudy, plain, would be glued together to create mosaics, mosaics that depicted scenes from Greek mythology. The works went on show at the Mediterranean Art Gallery in the small town of Caphos on the island and they usually attracted quite a lot of attention and plaudits. Giorgios, the artist-diver and the leader of the three, was as magisterial and driven as a cheetah; he had even written a book detailing his passion for shells and for their transformation into details in works of art, painstakingly and lovingly assembled. He also ran a taverna with Dora, his wife and fellow diver who was floating close by him. She reached out an ungloved hand to touch the skin-like surface of the shell. She smiled through her mask and the couple executed a little dance of triumph. As they did this Kirsten, who was the youngest of the trio, felt a little displaced from them. They, after all, were bound by marital vows and the activity of their loins. Kirsten had no such connection to another human soul and was wary of people. Only in the sea, in its underwater chambers, in its caressing, silent embrace, did she feel truly complete, truly whole and peaceful. Up there, in the earthly world, in the terrestrial shell of noise and strife, life was heavy, and people made no sense, with their changing patterns of behaviour, contradictory, selfish, and sometimes downright cruel.

The divers began to rise, drifting upwards like elongated

shadows of birds borne skywards. They passed great gold corrugated leaves of macro-algae, moving slowly up and down like giant feather fans, palpitatingly alive. As the divers spiralled upwards towards the shimmering ceiling of light, small fish with black and yellow vertical stripes imitated the arc of their movements, almost as though setting up some wondrous homage to their human counterparts. Then the fish sped away, gone, vanishing into the secret places only they knew how to reach.

The divers, one by one, glided up to their small diving boat, and climbed up over the side by means of a small ladder, removing their gear and breathing apparatus and placing it on the stern. The sun was setting and the air was full of the heady vivid sensations of summer. Overhead the sky was beginning to fade to a pinkish red glow. The moon was already visible and Kirsten spied it with her furtive, shy eyes. How different this scene was to those of Kirsten's childhood and teenage years, before she had come to embrace her new Mediterranean life. English summers had only ever been at best a tepid affair; the temperature never rose above the twenties and the sky was more often than not a screen of clouds and greyness. She preferred this richer, more luscious backdrop, its subtle light, dying now, but all the more beautiful and poignant for it, the endless surface of the sea, ever changing, ever moving, but always a harbinger of calm and joy, the tiny vantage point afforded by their boat, and the salt air, which seemed to hold all the textures of life in its invisible embrace.

They started making their way back to shore, silent and slightly overwhelmed as they tended to be after a dive.

Kirsten said goodbye to the couple and walked over to her Volkswagen Beetle, dusty and battered in the sandy driveway that led down to the beach. The car had dents everywhere, as though serving as a visible reminder of Kirsten's lack of grace whenever she was out of water. As a child she had always been accumulating bruises and blisters and seemed to have a knack for harming herself: bumping her head, scraping her knee caps, falling off slides and breaking her wrist, her hip, her nose. Underwater everything was lighter, friction was robbed of its power to hurt, weight was dissipated. Maybe that was why she loved to dive . . .

She drove back to the village, where she was staying at a villa that the parents of her friend Melissa had bequeathed to her for a few days. The villa contained worlds of old-style grace, filled with ethereal pleasures that only Kirsten (she liked to think) was allowed to sample. From outside the simple beauty of the indigo-blue wooden front door with no lock, just a latch, tantalisingly hinted at the magical dimensions of what lay beyond its threshold. The door remained without a lock because the locals and the village still existed in a universe of guilelessness. In Caphos, everything slowed down, buses were late, coffee was sipped rather than swallowed, the souvlaki was cooked slowly, the hours passed slowly and it didn't matter because either the sun or the sea or something ensured that it was fine to do absolutely nothing and yet somehow it was never boring or oppressive. Life could be lived merely by observing, meditating, being.

The villa was a glorious gift to Kirsten and for three days she sampled all its delights, prising open its secrets: the magnificent view of the village down below and the rows and clusters of evening lights as they switched on magically; the breakfast room and kitchen, with its strangely modern sink, a burnished, smooth block of elegance; the unbelievably opulent plants and geraniums and bougainvillea, which she lovingly watered; the long, almost Victorian bathtub that was twice as long as she was; the summerhouse that adjoined the main body of the villa and, most wonderfully of all, the outdoor swimming pool, which she slipped into at midnight every night; a small, exquisite pool whose surface was hardly disturbed by the movements of her lithe, naked body, as she swam without sound, greedily clutching at those gowns of water, and wrapping them around her. She strove to become one with the water, to move in tireless, perfect patterns, as each stroke and each length she completed became a better and better embodiment of technique and elegance. There, in that midnight shrine, outside, as she floated on her back, looking up, she peered into the basin of the night sky and the constellations and clusters of stars were like freckles on the face of the universe. Here was the perfection she had dreamed of: a silky, almost erotic abundance of water, her own form dissolving, melting into it, almost becoming water in all its protean freedom, the natural scene around, where stones and flowers existed in symbiotic, breath-held harmony, as though reality had become an etched painting, and the vacuum of utter silence, far far away from noise and people. She swam in wonder and gratitude as the night reached out and made love to her.

2

A wild stretch of the shore with a small beach.

Close by clusters of rocks formed tiny islands that caught the sun's glare; children clambered over them, their parents stretched out on them. Inland, a complex of new, ugly apartments had just been built. Kirsten hated them. Far off, out to sea, the wreck of a ship was embedded in the horizon. A gargantuan Turkish freighter with a cargo of steel had struck the jagged rocks some fourteen years earlier and there it sat, a rusty, static monolith of decay. Tourists sighted it and wondered why it was always there day after day until someone pointed out that it would never move again. Something held Kirsten to the shipwreck, and she stared at it all the time she was down by the beach, with its wooden umbrellas and porkchop British tourists and leaden, unsmiling Russians. She stared at it for hours and sometimes shuddered at its dark form: an unmoving malevolent presence that, as the shadows of night gathered, became even darker and evocative of damnation. The perpetual stasis of this great decomposing entity seemed truly to carve an incision in the water. When Kirsten drove her car along the dust road, running parallel to the beach, but at an elevated point, she would always look out for the shipwreck. And it never failed to appear, it always came round eventually and, in a way, it had become part of the sea, even as it tarnished it, ensnared by the rocks with which it had begun to fuse. Kirsten began to feel that the secret of life lay hidden in that shipwreck, and gradually it occurred to her that she must somehow confront it, come face to face with it.

One warm, windy night when the moon was almost full, Kirsten took out the little diving boat and gradually drifted all the way out towards it, afraid and uncertain of what she would find there, but knowing that confronting her fear would bring her some kind of peace. She half expected to see grinning corpses. She stopped the boat some meters away from the shipwreck's orbit – a perpetually splashing foam around steel and rock – and stood, scared, hypnotised by that gigantic, cold, dead form towering above her and her tiny boat. She felt her skin crawl as some nameless dread gathered all around her. She stood frozen, trying to arrest even the tiniest of bodily movements, even her breathing, on the lookout for a predator that would leap out at her from the darkness. The moonlight caught patches of the watery membrane around her, and a dark beauty was born. Her boat inched forward. The waves snarled and crashed ever and again into the ship's derelict hull, as though trying to knock dents in it, and weird phantoms were made in that clash between dead metal and water, strange reverberations that scurried across the body of the freighter.

Kirsten felt her skin grow cold and clammy; adrenaline was shooting through every part of her. She pulled out her torch and pointed it at the ship. She could make out a large rip in the metal and she flashed her beam into it, and inside a cold, abandoned world was revealed. It was as if the curtains of a theatre had parted only to reveal nothing, an illusion, for behind that façade was mere emptiness, the interior of the ship had long since been stripped and scooped out like the innards of an eviscerated fish. All that remained was the terrible shell of the exterior, locked into the rocky matrix below that had seized it and would never relinquish it. She moved her boat in closer, then closer still until it was shuddering in the waves. She dropped the anchor, so the craft was secured. Her boat slapping against the freighter (it seemed to stretch to infinity), she staggered over to the stern and, craning forward, passed both her hands through the great rip in the hull. Her hands and then her arms had slipped through to the other side, and she spread out all her fingers, placed her ear against the cold hard metal wall and listened. The waves smashing against the ship boomed in her eardrum; the sound was magnified, colossal; it plunged into Kirsten like groping tentacles. She was engulfed in reverberating sound; sound compressed her every fibre. She was deafened, stupefied. She felt as though her body were a conductor of energy, and she had been plugged into the universe's nameless current, and now it was coursing, coruscating through her, through her bones, her heart, her arteries, her brain.

What was it that lay on the other side? Why was she putting herself through this mad experience? What was she trying to find? Maybe it was the final day, that expires in night with no hope of a remedying sunrise, its cleansing hand thrust into the corners of gloom and murk, lifting both as the purifying light exiles all shadows. Maybe she sought an everlasting dusk, a cessation of the senses? She wanted to pass through to the other side, to say that she had dwelled inside that vacuum there. But finally she could stand it no more and she moved her ear away from the hull and pulled her arms back, half surprised that her hands were still attached to them. As if unleashed by her liberation the wind blew up with hurricane force, the waves climbed and lashed out and engulfed the boat in foam which was instantly dissipated and created anew as the water continued to bludgeon the deck with sudden unbelievable ferocity. Trembling violently, she flopped back into the boat – pitching wildly in the undertow – and there she lay flattened out and drenched, incapable of movement or speech or even thought. She was half dead, caught in the vortex; the sea had been tied into a knot, she lay suspended within it, and was rattled about in its inexhaustible epicentre ...

But at last she regained a fragment of strength, and crawled on her hands and knees over to the tiller and started up the engine. She activated the electric anchor winch to free the boat, and the craft moved off. Almost at once the sea started to level out as the wind subsided. Everything grew miraculously quiet after the din of the waves. In the distance she could make out small dots of lights scattered along the shore and she was heartened by them as she took the wheel. With her gaze fixed steadfastly on the lights, the waves of terror subsided and she felt safe, almost protected.

She felt she had done enough, she could go back. She had proven something, confronted the uncharted terror of life's underbelly. The boat was beginning to reach the shore. Kirsten had the energy now to begin emptying out the water swirling around the deck, with the aid of a small bucket. A text message came through on her mobile phone, which was strange as there was no signal out there. It was from Dora, asking if she wanted to go diving tomorrow. She suddenly felt like she knew something the perfect couple didn't, and finally had a story of her own to tell, that she had dived deeper than they had this time. Brushing these thoughts aside, she remembered the midnight swim at the villa that was waiting for her and this imbued her with a feeling of almost physical warmth. She moored the boat and scooped out the remaining water.

Inside the cabin, Kirsten took a few minutes to collect herself. She glugged down some water, dried her hair and legs, and changed into jeans and a salmon pink, gauzy blouse. On glancing in the mirror she thought she looked shaken, so she splashed her face, dabbed herself with Kleenex, and put on some bright scarlet lipstick, smoothing her lips evenly. She combed her hair carefully, almost with love. And she noticed that these actions, which normally did not come easily to her and often ended in disaster, were rather enjoyable. She took another look at herself and murmured, 'Not bad, but you can do better', upended the contents of her bag, found a necklace with a silver-plated shark's tooth and put it on, and its icy, refined beauty was accentuated in the flimsiness of her blouse. Then she dabbed her wrists and cheeks with perfume. She was ready now.

As she walked along the shore she noticed that her heart was still beating very quickly; it was taking a long time for her to come back down to normal. Some way down the beach there was a little bar, whose rows of fairy lights announced it. She ordered an ouzo, and sipped it, beginning to feel better. A few old unshaven Greeks were playing backgammon, a giant TV screen sat in an ugly corner, some small children splashed in a water pool. Two men in their twenties were smoking cigarettes and chatting easily. They wore ripped jeans and were tanned. They both had a cultivated, intelligent air and they sipped coffees and shared a plate of baklava. It was as different a situation to the one she had just been in as was possible to imagine. She was filled with a sweet exhaustion combined with the residual joy that had slipped through the meshes of overwhelming physical exertion and fear, and life was ineffably sweet. The beautiful surroundings, the ocean that was hers, the future beckoning with its promise of as yet unsampled pleasures, and the possibility of love: it was as if she had just been handed a menu filled with subtle, exquisite dishes. At that moment nothing would have saddened or vexed her.

Would she go diving tomorrow with Dora and Giorgios?

She wasn't sure. She wondered if the two men – now sizing her up with remarkably undisguised interest – could have guessed what she'd just been doing. They could tell that at that moment Kirsten was light, was on the point of rising upwards. And when she flashed them both a smile they were caught off guard, not knowing whether to be embarrassed or to be encouraged or to be self-conscious or to be charmed so they both ended up being all of these. Kirsten's eyes were bursting at that moment with something, a mischievous affection for these young men, an unaccountable love for them which was totally at odds with their status as complete strangers. As she watched them and wondered about them she concluded that they were clean-cut, sweet guys who were already totally in awe of her and of her mood at the moment in which they had all happened to intersect. She could tell that they were so in awe that they would never have dreamt of starting a conversation or walking over to her. She thought about this for a while, still watching them from afar, and then at last she decided that it was up to her so she knocked back the rest of her ouzo and strode over and the way she moved across the floor was blazingly provocative, rocking her hips and bottom, and she half pouted and half grinned and then she pulled up a chair and sat down and said softly, 'Hallo, I'm Kirsten. My hands were just inside a shipwreck.'

# ERASING THE WAVES

So here I am, riding on a tiny wave that keeps faltering and ebbing uncertainly until at last it is absorbed into the tide which is now as flat and rigid as gelatine. My wave is like a myopic, old man trying to thread a needle. No, let's say he has glaucoma. You get the picture, if you'll excuse the pun. There's this old fart and he's half blind, has lost half his marbles and he's trying to get this thread through a needle. What are the chances? Millions to one? Maybe not millions, but it's tough, and the day is long and the sun is harsh and I am tired. How can I get that wave to rise again like some old prince, once exiled, now returned, bearing all his treasures, his subjects bowing down in adoration? It's no good, that wave is never going to make it; it's been lost in the tide as flat and rigid as gelatine.

Ten years ago was the last time I saw him; ten years is a long time, but not for someone like me who has squandered his life and ruined his mind with drugs, drink, porn, and procrastination.

Procrastination. Not only is it the thief of time, it's also the assassin of time, it's the hit man of time. Too much of it will kill you. I'd heard that he'd hit the big time and was making movies in Hollywood, hobbing with the rich and nobbing the famous. What does it take, I ask myself, to bed the famous? Does it require levels of conversational brilliance that ordinarily might lead to a cardiac arrest? Would it require, in my case, plastic surgery, the hot wiring of a Ferrari, a wallet full of credit cards and a phonebook full of influential people's numbers? It's not that I aspire towards such things as such, I just sit back and drop my jaw when I consider those who have them, those who have managed to access the never regions of the golden divas and the fifteen-foot high-screen goddesses.

When we'd last met he was writing adverts. For mindless clients with more money than sense. I was in London working as a freelance journalist. Freelance means unemployed for ninety per cent of the time. The rest is taken up in anxiety, making phone calls to people who don't want to speak to you, and waiting for calls from people who will never ring. In the years that passed I limped along on a penny farthing while Aaron – that was his name, by the way – drove along country roads, then motorways, then motorways in Germany with no speed limits, and then traded his car for a spaceship until finally he was blasting off to other solar systems. He knew how to do it all right, the old tinker, snake charmer: immaculate suits, slicked back hair. It wasn't enough that he was getting to do what he loved and being paid astronomical sums of money for it, it wasn't enough that he was sleeping with fantastic women whose sexual energy could have launched the space shuttle, he also had to have matinee-idol looks and perfect grooming. When I wake up, I resemble something that has recently been deposited in a morgue, whereas Aaron's quirks and stubble serve to enhance his handsome looks and poise.

By an odd series of circumstances, I found myself re-connecting with Aaron. We used to live together at university and had at one time been quite close. In those days we subsisted on pasta, baked beans on toast and the occasional sausage. Now, ten years later and he had decided to take me out for dinner at the kind of establishment where the price tag requires you to remortgage your home.

When he came into the restaurant I recognised him, but at the same time he looked different. His physiognomy was the same, but his altogether new aura of success and confidence if not empirically, at least expressionistically, altered him.

Actually moments before I had been thinking of a landscape in Mexico I had once seen. Its desolation. The thing about desolation – but only when it manifests itself within a sun-drenched setting like a Mexican desert with cacti and infinite skies and the derelict backended fragments of an abandoned bus or abandoned house or bus shelter that has been melted by the sun – the thing about that particular brand of desolation is that it arrests the unarrestable mind, brings to a grinding halt the mind's relentless motion, finally vaporizes the memories, impressions, fragments that uneasily bustle together in that cracked mortar. And standing there in that desert so many years ago I had seen, or thought I had seen, a women emerge from out of the shadows of a broken bus, young and svelte and sexy as hell; she'd seen me, or thought she had, but a moment later she was gone, and another women sleepwalked her way out of that same bus, and she was fat and old and ugly as hell and it was the same woman or not the same and in the interval between that first woman and that second woman years had passed in seconds so that I had jumped forward to the first woman's eventual transformation into the second by virtue of a wormhole that brought together two opposing moments from her youth and middle age.

These were the kind of crazy things going through my

head when Aaron strode in. He grinned and came up to me and took my hand. I fell in love. Platonically. I had never been in love with him in the first place but now I was. Maybe I was just star-struck, or maybe he was so beguiling, with his fame and success and confidence that I fell for him, big time, fell for the image, the razzmatazz, the whole package.

'What's your poison?' he asked. 'I'll have the same.'

That was Aaron. The way he could make you feel accepted, make you feel that he wanted to be like you, that you were the one setting the rules, which he was content to follow, whereas he was the one really leading the way through his larger-than-life command, his benign banishing of doubt. If he were to don a dozen disguises of wildly differing appearance, one would always recognise Aaron behind them, whereas someone with a lesser personality would become buried, submerged, and eventually invisible.

'It's good to see you. After all this time. And other clichés,' I said. He smiled broadly and placed a lean hand inside his pocket.

'I've got something for you. It's a ticket. I have a new film coming out. I want you to come to the premiere.'

Of course, I thought, of course he has a new film; for him it's as habitual as a new haircut is for others.

'I think you'll find it interesting.'

'I'd be delighted.'

I suppose I had never been around a really famous person before. It sort of does odd things to you: you find yourself eager to please, eager to laugh, eager to turn yourself into a caricature of yourself, eager to recognise names you've never heard of, eager to disappear. We ordered and the courses arrived and the conversation was taken up largely with reminiscences about our days together, the memorable characters we had known, tales about Hollywood and the insanity of the scene there, the pressure on studio executives to come up with hits, the pressure on actors to look eternally young and trim, and the absolute garbage that millions of dollars were squandered on. I wanted to ask him about the women, but felt it would have been inappropriate. In the old days such a question would have been absolutely normal, but now his fame prevented me from asking anything too direct. Besides, I didn't want him to think that I was fishing around for titbits that I might later sell to the toxic lowlife carcinogenic vermin amoral scumbags otherwise known as tabloid journalists. As we talked, he laughed uproariously at some of my comments, and I could tell it was genuine laughter and that he was actually enjoying being with me after all this time. At a certain point after we had consumed a fair amount of wine, he dropped his guard and entered a new groove of relaxation.

'You know, it's really great to see you again. I've thought about you many times over the years.'

'You've thought about *me*? Really?'

I have to admit I was flattered.

'Sure I did. You made a big impression on me.'

'I did? But I'm such a big zero, such a nobody.'

'Don't talk like that. That's not true. You just haven't found your niche yet.'

I was silent.

'You know, it's so great just to sit here and get pissed with you and not have to always be performing or doing PR stunts or be in control or be the one with all the answers and the 24-carat-gold ideas and the solutions.'

His hand went to his nose and he pressed his fingers

downwards into his abdomen. Something about the movement struck me as redolent of anxiety. He did it again and it occurred to me that it was like some kind of nervous tic.

'Why are you telling me this, Aaron?' I asked.

'I don't know. Because you're normal, because you won't judge me, or at least I hope you won't. Because I don't have to pretend everything is hunky dory and that I can walk on water and levitate and turn water into a barrel of gin and tonic, I guess.'

We both laughed. It was fascinating to see him unwind.

'I must admit I'm surprised,' I said.

'By what?'

'By your candour.'

'No.'

I looked at him. His hand went to his stomach again.

'That's not what's surprising you,' he said. 'It's not my candour, it's my show of vulnerability. Wouldn't you agree?'

I smiled, he was right.

'Well, I suppose I wasn't expecting to see that side of you. Or maybe I thought that side didn't exist.'

'Why not?'

'Come on, Aaron. You know what I mean.'

He said nothing. For the first time I had a fear of the evening going wrong or ending in recrimination or tension, which was not what I wanted.

I spoke lightly. 'Come on, I mean, look at your life, you've got it all. You're a respected film director who makes commercial movies that are actually great films as well. You live in LA, you're surrounded by fantastic woman, the critics are in love with you, you're free to make the films in the way that you want to make them. You have incredible talent. Need I go on?'

He said nothing for a moment or two. Then he smiled and the mood lifted.

'Yes, I suppose when you put it like that it does sound quite good. But I could lose it all. I could make a turkey, the critics could crucify me. I could screw up big time.'

'I suppose . . . But so could we all. Look at me. I fucked up long ago. Feeling vulnerable : it occupies a fleeting moment of your day, but forms the habitual texture of mine. Know what I mean?'

'I'm sorry to hear that.'

'I know you are.'

I reached for the wine bottle and refilled his glass generously. It's always a good idea to engage in some kind of physical activity during awkward moments.

'So how about it, Aaron? What's the secret? How did you manage it?'

'I don't know. A lot of it is luck, you have to understand that.'

'And what is luck?'

'Luck is like a level crossing when a train's about to arrive. The lights start to flash, the barriers come down. Then the train arrives. Then the train goes and the barriers go up. For most of the time the barriers are up, the lights don't flash, maybe you'd be forgiven for thinking that there's a level crossing at all. But luck is when the lights keep on flashing and the trains just keep coming. Eventually after you've had so much luck you get catapulted onto a place where you no longer require it. That's when the barriers part and you can finally drive.'

'But, to follow your analogy, the trains keep coming and the barriers are down. So that would suggest that luck is blocking you?'

'No. The luck is protecting you from getting injured, just like the barriers protect you from being mowed down by a train.'

His hand went to his nose. It was an interesting idea, though I wasn't entirely convinced.

'Aaron, can I ask you a question?'

'Go ahead.'

'Do you have a cocaine habit?'

'Oh, I see, the nose. No, I have a pimple inside my nostril and it's really bothersome. Disgusting, isn't it? Please don't tell anyone.'

'You have my word, as a gentleman.'

I swallowed a hefty gulp of wine. I worried that the evening was reaching its conclusion and that soon he would announce his departure and the prospect of it pained me.

'Where do you get your ideas?' I asked.

'Good question. Haven't figured that one out yet.'

'Do you keep a notepad?'

'Hey, what's this turning into? An interview?' He managed a simultaneous frown and a smile, a smown, if you will.

'No, of course not, I'm just curious.'

'Well, you know, it's like anything: periods of fertility, periods of stagnation. I've had my moments of stagnation, believe me.'

'Somehow I don't.'

'I thought not.'

'What's been the worst?'

'Oh, I've had my bad moments.'

'Care to discuss them?'

'Well . . . maybe after some more wine.'

'Ok, fair enough, I wouldn't want you to feel like you're

walking the plank or anything. Christ, I'm shot Aaron, I swear I'm not normal. Is it possible to die of excessive masturbation?'

'I wouldn't have thought so.' We laughed and it was easy. I recalled our old student days: slow punts down the Wear, the occasional philosophical problem, and an hour at best of studying in the Palace Green library. In those long-gone days of university, Aaron and I would spend the small hours chatting and smoking, putting the world's problems to rights, dreaming up ways to seduce girls with names like Catherine Fudge and Laura Rowly-Williams. The long summer appeared like a well-kept promise, and on the green students played crochet and made tits of themselves, while I sat at the side unobserved, writing, and drinking tea from pint jugs.

Aaron stared hard into my eyes.

'What do you want from life?' he asked.

'Christ. What a question. What does anyone want? To survive, I suppose.'

'Is that all? Mere survival?'

'Well, I gave up on my dreams, or they gave up on me.'

'You wanted to be a writer? Of fiction?'

'Indeed, yes, I wanted to make things up for a living until it rapidly became clear no one was interested in publishing what I made up.'

'But there's still a light within you, you are still brilliant and witty and even at times imperturbable.'

'That's kind of you. But failure is my real calling.'

'Come on, don't talk like that.'

'Well, you know, I just feel kind of washed up.'

'Accept defeat, get washed up with all the fucking seaweed and beer cans, then start again. Never give up though. Fight.

Fight the bastards until you prove them wrong. Go into the battle, not weary and dry, but with all guns blazing. Fail again.'

'Fail better,' I added. We both smiled at the Beckett quotation.

'Exactly. Every film I make is a failure, every film I finish is imperfect. That's what keeps me going: the drive to create something great, truly great.'

'You don't regard your films as great?'

'Come on, I'm middlebrow, I've never going to make *The Apartment* or *Blade Runner* or *Eight and a Half*. One has to accept one's limitations. Maybe it's just not possible in today's world to do something lofty, something really great. You know why? Because we've become allergic to greatness. We're afraid that it will expose us, reveal our inner emptiness. So we churn out shit, because shit is the medium of our age, just like blank verse was the medium of Shakespeare's age and the long novel was the medium of the nineteenth century.'

'Do you really think that?'

'Pretty much.'

'Somehow I don't believe you. You know what you do isn't shit. I know that what I do isn't shit. But I haven't the foggiest clue what the others think of what I do, or what they do, or what anyone does. But when I'm lying on my deathbed, I want to look back on something concrete, something final and polished. Some kind of body of work that I can say I was proud of, even if it ends up stuck in a drawer or, these days, on a hard drive.'

'That's the spirit, keep the flame burning. I know you know you're good, that you have something to say. Keep on saying it, keep on singing.'

Despite myself I was moved – his sincerity and his tenderness and his mercurial belief buoyed me, I felt less alone, sustained by his understanding and solidarity. The storm clouds seemed to recede, the sun's rays cut through the rain and there was some kind of transition, in my mind or in reality or in the fabric of consciousness.

Aaron took a drop of wine.

'There was this girl I used to love. I loved her in a way that was different. I loved her, I really did. But she didn't love me back. She was with another man. The way I loved her . . . it's hard to imagine. If she had been wearing a dress, I would have loved her in that dress. If she had been wearing overalls, I would have loved her in those overalls, if she had been wearing a piece of string, I would have loved her in string. And I would have loved her dress, her overalls, her string. Just to hear her voice was bliss, just to touch her hand was bliss. I loved her so much that the love transcended the pain of her rejection of me. I loved her so much that it propelled me onto a place where there is no love, where there is no pain, because I had found she gave me a view of the universe, cosmic, complete.'

'God. What happened to her?'

'She faded. Faded away. Like people do. But we let them fade. We let them go. That love, that was really something, a real demonstration of the eternal indefatigable affirmation of being, the sleight of hand that reveals the void that is all, everything and nothing, birth and death, life beamed onto your retina, a paraffin lamp swinging in heaven's guest room. If that's not fucking inspiring, I don't know what is.'

What a guy – he was even sensitive, he could even extemporise around the old unrequited refrain, jam like all the best poets and drunks, squandering their rich souls on women who would never cough up. He was that good, that cool, that big.

'The worst thing is not to feel; the worst thing is a flat, barren existence, devoid of pain, devoid of joy, a tepidness that makes you sink into the marshland. You've got me talking now, waxing lyrical, or waxing hysterical. Kind of.'

I looked around me – the restaurant's opulent surroundings, the other diners savouring the delights of their deserts. Everything seemed fine, the world was ordered, pleasurable. It seemed inconceivable to dwell on life's burdens and disappointments. For a moment I was free. I wished that this moment might somehow extend to embrace all of life.

'Keep talking Aaron, keep talking, it's gold dust.'

'Thanks, you're very kind.'

'You talk, I'll listen.'

He sat back in his chair and adjusted his jacket. He ran his fingers through his hair and seemed to hesitate. I noticed an attractive woman in a kimono at another table glance over in his direction. Perhaps she recognised him, perhaps she had caught some of our conversation and found it interesting. It was difficult to say. I would have liked to have invited her over. But how? I couldn't see a way. So, she would be lost, like ten thousand other women who go into the night and are never seen or heard from again. And yet, sometimes just a slight thing, a flicker of recognition, a well-chosen compliment administered at the right moment, and ... well ... People can forge links in moments, in moments nestled between eternities of waiting, of loneliness, of expectation. At once I saw how tenuous everything was, how fragile, of how unrehearsed life was. Spoken words were like forms and shapes drawn in the air, possessing no weight, no dimensionality, gestures were forgotten, the present tense, the present moment was a perpetual flight from fixity, collapsing into memory, into abstraction, like a plane that breaks apart as its engines fail and it plummets, screeching towards the earth.

'What was her name, the woman you were speaking about?'

'Oh, it's not important. What possible meaning can a name have? I could tell you her name, I could describe her face, I could even show you a photo, but none of it would matter, none of it would be able to evoke the sensations I experienced when I was with her or when I thought about her. You know what I mean?'

I nodded slowly and smiled with re-booted charisma. I smiled to show him that I understood, that I knew what he was talking about, to let him know that with me he didn't have to pretend, to go through the motions, to utter platitudes. And in that moment we were back, back where we had been before, in the old days, back in the place of quiet understanding and camaraderie. He glanced over to one of the roaming waiters and signalled for the bill.

'You know,' he began, 'for a long time, my career just wasn't happening. No one wanted to know me, I couldn't get any funding for a short film, let alone a feature film. I was making shitty little commercials. I was pretty depressed and taking different medications. The idea of doing my first movie seemed like light years away. I worshipped the greats, Wilder, Quenebec, Herzog, but when I watched their films I felt like I was at the bottom of a ravine and that there was no way of climbing back. Soon even the adverts started to dry up and no one had any time for my pitches. My agents in Paris and London didn't return my calls. My producer was always tied up with something else. I started drinking. The money was running out. I asked my dad for a loan, but he refused me point blank. He was a military man and in his eyes I had failed, so why should he bankroll a failure? So, there I was, waking up at twelve, helping myself to a beer for breakfast and by night time I was so drunk I could barely stand. I knew that soon it would all be over. Unless something major happened, or someone called with a real job. I had nothing and no one wanted to know me or help me. Much like the opposite of today.

'One night I got drunk but not too drunk and decided to go for a walk. At that time I was living in a bedsit in Tufnell Park. I decided to head for Canary Wharf. It was epic and the night was cold. My head was spinning with thoughts of suicide. I remember that as I walked, everything looked alien to me – the black cabs with their yellow illuminated TAXI signs seemed especially odd and frightening, strange insects droning through the night. The cold streets of London were deserted. Each bar I passed seemed uninviting and lonely. The red post boxes and phone booths were like discarded parts of a sterile landscape. My mind seemed to have fallen apart and my thoughts were racing, but I tried to slow them down and bring back some order.

'Whichever way I looked at it, my problems seemed unsolvable. No one wanted my work anymore, I felt it in my bones, I just knew that they weren't interested in me. I had had a brief moment of success when people were knocking at the door, but the knocks had become more and more infrequent and now there was just silence. I had tried so hard but it wasn't happening anymore and there was no use swimming against the current. It was just too strong. I really felt that I was at the end, penniless, with zero prospects.

'As I turned the corner – I don't remember exactly where I was, but it was somewhere near Blackfriars, I remember the Thames was illuminated by moonshine and one or two colossal ships were carved into it, I started to think about what it would feel like to drown. But the thought of dipping into the freezing waters of the Thames was too awful to contemplate. I pushed on without paying much attention to my surroundings and after a while realised that I was completely lost and had ended up in some maze of small alleyways. Further up there was a dead end so I decided to turn back. The night was getting colder and at that moment I would have liked nothing more than to have stepped into a nice warm pub and ordered a pint of ale, but the place was deserted and everywhere was barred and bolted. I gave up on the idea of finding someone who might be able to direct me. Anyway I managed to find my way to a main road that I didn't recognise, crossed it and found myself at a large council housing estate. Nearby there was an intersection so I crossed over and then turned a corner and found myself in what looked like a private road. There was a white stucco house, quite grand and from it came sounds of voices and music, which gave me a kind of boost.

'I stood there, freezing, huddled into my coat, wondering what the hell to do. Then a couple of men, they were both dressed in pretty expensive winter coats, straight out of Jermyn Street, I would say, appeared out of nowhere and walked straight up to me. They looked pretty civilised so I didn't think anything of it. I thought that one of them was going to ask me for a cigarette. He spoke very clearly, I remember, and said, "What are you doing here?" "Nothing, just taking a walk." "Walk somewhere else." I kind of imagined that I must have been intruding on private property or the scene of some kind of illegal activity. I noticed that one of the men had a strong accent. I guessed it to be Ukrainian or Latvian. "I'll walk where I like," I said, not really afraid. It was more that I felt numb, indifferent. A second or two must have passed. Nothing happened. He just stared at me with a very cold, hard expression in his eyes. It's difficult to describe it but he didn't really appear human to me at that moment. It was almost as if he was like some incredibly sophisticated replica of a human being or a waxwork model. I felt this phenomenally tight sensation near my abdomen and couldn't understand what had happened. I clutched my side and the warm stickiness of my own blood. "Come on man," he said, "you know, you wanted it, you were looking for it. I was just doing you a favour. I took one look at you and could see it in your eyes."

'As I fell to the ground my eyes grew dim and I saw the two of them walking away, just as if nothing had happened. I lay there for a moment or two, blood spilling out of me all over the ground. And then the pain started. It really came into its own. The only way I can describe it is it's as though someone is holding a cricket bat and slamming it repeatedly into you. I looked up and I remember that there were one or two stars in the sky and they seemed very bright. It was strange, I thought, that life was going on as usual around me, and that the world hadn't noticed anything; hadn't noticed my imminent expiry. I lost consciousness briefly, then woke to find the agony greater than ever. I felt that I had leapt ever closer to death and that I didn't have that much time left. I suddenly had the sense that this close-up of death was what I had needed all along. But now I was too close and about to pass through to the other side. The other man, not the one who'd stabbed me, was coming back. I thought he'd come back to finish off the job. He was very big this guy and obviously extremely strong. He lifted me up and held me in his arms like a broken doll. I was beginning to black out again. My memory of what happened next is vague. He stuffed me into a car. I remember some sounds like bells. Or maybe a mobile phone was ringing. I was aware of the motion of the car as it drove. And then whatever happened after that is gone.

'I woke up in hospital in a ward with six or seven other patients and my mother was sitting there, overjoyed to see me open my eyes. I spent some time talking to the police, but they never found the guy who did it to me. My impression was they just kind of gave up on the case after a few months. I spent two weeks in hospital and I must say I rather enjoyed being fussed over and pampered. My father came to see me and told me that things would be different from now on and that he would help me out with any money I might need. It all felt very unreal and alien to me, like I was in a film. Every now and then my mind would drift off and I would just kind of zone out and feel like I wasn't there. But as my wounds began to heal, normality returned. My stomach, the wounds, had to be dressed every day, and that was quite a performance. But I realised what a tireless capacity the body has for re-invention. It can survive almost anything and it can smooth over the cavities, the incisions. Sitting there in that bed I had time, time to think. Time to review my life. Time to review my almost death. And time to review the connection between the two. When you are that close to death, life becomes beautiful beyond words. Life becomes crystalline. And the angels – all of a sudden you can hear their voices, you can discern their forms, hovering, moving like tongues of flame. Peace, real peace. I found it there. I began to write. I wrote treatments for three screenplays. I sketched out scenes and wrote character sketches. I wrote with a freedom that I'd never known. Whole blocks of text just fell out of me as if I was taking dictation. Dictation from some external source.

'What seemed like decades later I got back to my flat in Tufnell Park. I'd only been in hospital for a fortnight, but I found it hard to remember what day it was or how much time had passed. I think some part of my mind had been shut down, so that everything was out of sync. You know that sudden jumping across valleys of time that occurs in sleep, when you think you've slept an hour but it's actually only a minute, something similar happened to me but while I was awake. I think the part of my brain that handles memory had been temporarily damaged. I felt like I was permanently jet-lagged. I would wake up at five in the morning and want to eat hamburgers or a steak or a prawn cocktail, or go to sleep at 1 p.m. and wake at midnight to start the day. This went on for weeks until finally I started to slip back into the usual rhythms of night and day. I continued writing and the writing was miraculously easy. I hardly even needed to make notes or plot anything – it all just took care of itself. Then one day, I guess this would have been a month after the stabbing, the phone rang. It hadn't rung in weeks and I hadn't told anyone about what had happened to me. At first I ignored it, hoping it would stop, but then I picked it up. It was my London agent. He told me he had some great news: Nike wanted me for their new campaign and were willing to fly me out to Shanghai the next day. The pay was incredibly good. For a moment I hesitated and thought about turning down the job. But I said yes.

'Shortly after that my agent received a call from someone in Los Angeles who was interested in meeting me and discussing a script he'd been sitting on for a year.

'Well, that's the way it panned out. I can't really explain it. I don't really know what it all means. But my guess is that someone or something decided that I'd been through enough and that it was time for me to get a break. Maybe there was a connection between that night and the subsequent flowering of my career. Or maybe there wasn't. I'll leave that to you to decide. I like to think there was, but maybe that's just the romantic in me. By the way, I'd be grateful if you didn't share that story with anyone else, particularly since it's true.'

I sat there. The wine was finished. All the other diners seemed to have gone home.

'That's amazing,' I mumbled.

Aaron just smiled. For a tiny moment I had the feeling he was going to say that in fact he'd made the whole thing up. As though reading my mind, he lifted his shirt and showed me a network of complex scars running along his stomach.

'Just in case you had any doubts . . .' he said.

I thought of the women in Mexico, coming out of the bus, time leaping, and dissolving like waves lapping ever and again on a distant shore.

# ISLAND

I

And she did a second later.

※

She was sleek and classy and imperturbable, dressed all in black: a black Trilby, black cashmere coat, black scarf, black brogues and black leotard. She sped past like a land speeder, a layer of air between her and the floor, when the en-masse dancing began, the unruly dancing, after a bit of belly dancing, which was the skilled dancing, the artifice and ritual seeping out into the night and arresting the movement of cigarette smoke, stopping it short so that it had to shut down, freeze, fall over itself. She seemed to be the one in command, she seemed to be choreographing the whole thing, like the person behind the scenes, off stage, who retains all the power. She was untouchable, she ran with the wolves, she soared with the angels, she shot up with the junkies, she did it all, her effortless wolf whistles full blooded and blood curdling and drawn out, giving subtle nods of assent and acknowledgement to the dancers. Was she orchestrating it all? Was she behind it all? Was she conning everyone with electric charisma, making fools of the establishment, the experts? She moved with the music, she seemed to have all the answers, she was that serpentine perfection that philosophers write about, that artists dream of, that composers extract music from. And then . . . after I had looked away and before I could form words, she had gone, vanished as though she had never existed in the first place. I had a ghostly recollection of a virtuoso barman, crafting expert cocktails with tentacles instead of hands, but no such barman existed apparently.

When it was all over and the place was trashed with shattered plates and half destroyed tables and streamers and empty bottles, I could tell it was late, God it was late, my flesh still stirred in the expiring search for more pleasure. The end was ignominious, squalid, drunken couples passed out, having abandoned attempts at coitus, the evening like a bottle of champagne that had long gone flat, the night a dried prune employed to quench the thirst of an old man who gropes in vain for his reading glasses and then, in his blindness, ends up pulverising them underfoot.

On the island, time didn't really exist in the usual sense. In the company of transcendental sunsets and exquisite food and backdrops of eternity rendered tangible, it was easy to forget about time, it was easy to forget about seconds and hours and days. One would sit in the Okala restaurant dining leisurely at midnight, sampling the kleftiko, which was so tender and molten that it was hard to imagine it was actually meat. My dinner companion was usually none other than a cat. A tiny thing, malnourished, underweight, emaciated, and yet the more I fed it, the more desperate and needy it seemed, until finally I dropped her the carcass, which she polished off, leaving only an immaculate bone. She slinked off and promptly, seamlessly, a dog slid into her place and took over, enticed by the smell of bone, and the dog gnawed at it until the bone was gone.

In those days, in that place, it wasn't painful or elegiac to dine alone, it was in the natural order of things, in fact everything that might have been a source of consternation slipped into the Adriatic like a seagull. In the prodigious blaze of Grecian sunlight, I was a cloud drifting, a god upon a lotus leaf, pondering the immensity of creation, no longer burdened by the need to understand, no longer lashed by six of the best, the imperative, the great corrugated WHY. It was in the air, this sublime release from thought, and I was wafting in the vacuum that is the now, the alpha and the omega, the front seat in the wings, the riff of the guitar solo that fades as the theatre and stadium and the freeway melt . . . falling off the edge of the precipice to find I'd sustained no injuries, waking to the perfume of all the lovers I'd lost, put through the shredder only to emerge later with all bodily parts intact and a more crystalline acoustic that brought me the music of the spheres. I'd switched from ginger beer to Guinness, from camomile tea to cappuccino, from nothing to being.

So there I was on the edge of the sea, the edge of infinity, the thing that struck me about this panorama without a name is . . . . The igloo-like houses, hewn out of caves maybe, out of earth, clay roasted in God's pipe – he must always be sleeping, snoozing, the old codger scrambling about for some painkillers, something to get him through the night. Maybe he stirs from time to time, disturbed by the acrid smell of blood from history. It keeps on being shed but God is too busy catching up on his kip to give a real damn so it's left to me to clean up the plasma with my mop and bucket but I just can't mop fast enough. So what do I do? Have another ouzo, have another smoke, look into the skyline, the heavens, the white

## Island

cliffs persist, bordered by pinpoints of clean, yellow lights, and here street lamps, dwarf level street lamps, attached to clean white edifices, flood my mind, and I notice, gradually it hits me that, beyond the sea, the houses, the cliffs, there is nothing, no trappings of tired civilisation, it's all so pure, so stopped, there are no adverts, no cars, no black smog factories, no unravelling intestines and umbilical cords still gooey with the bile of rhetoric and politicians' radioactive slime, no crowds, no newspapers, no hair extensions, I am in a balloon, floating free, in oxygenated space. Champagne cocktails flow into the drip that's hooked up to me and the nurses are all sexy or from the Ukraine or Sweden.

A French-looking man comes in, secretes himself into a bar that I'd slipped into earlier, after the kleftiko and the cat, but before sleep and dreams. He is with an ensemble of women and he looks like a film director, he wears the *8 and a half* hat, the women buzz around him like flies round a cowpat, he is effortless, his cigarette dangles. He laps it all up and sends them on their way, gives them his blessings, heals them like Christ, his phallus anointing them all with his sperm which they gratefully lap up on the shores of the Feminine Sea, still roaring and crashing and smashing. (That sea, by the way, takes my tiny little ego and drowns me good and proper, gives me a good old-fashioned dose of asphyxiation, whispers to me: hey little guy, poor bastard, you thought you could compete with this? You thought you could withstand this? All this pussy and labia and lips and tits and ass? You're just a tiny raft in the Ocean of Cunt, shortly to be snapped in two by the onslaught of vaginal waves.) So this French Fellini, this Danny Day Lewis type, these really fantastic women surrounding him, he really seems to be on a roll, he knows how to behave around them, he handles them as Stirling Moss would an Aston Martin. Tyres screech, smoke burns.

Then, in a lucid moment, I search for the choreographer but she's gone, she's hitched a slow ride with the boat to China.

On the island, time isn't the enemy anymore, it's become your friend, it resembles a fat, balding, short electrician who always wears a woollen hat. Each time you see this clown he looks the same, his leathery skin bearing no stigmata, no wrinkles. So you go up to him, chew the fat, and he tells you everything's just tickety-boo and he unveils a supply of days that is endless in July, what with the pristine light, the Greek coffee and the haloumi, and the baklava, and the idiotic tourists who you've begun to love in your unconditional-love frame of mind, and the wine and the ouzo and the long legs constantly sliding out from the sleek skirts, and the glimpses of tanned, supple backs promising to arch later at the touch of your third-degree-burn hand, and the island sleeps in the night, the single still-open bar somewhere out there, like an antechamber in heaven, with its white drapes reminiscent of an art installation, like a dentist's waiting room where the mouthwash is actually absinthe.

I continued to think about the choreographer. In my mind I shot a movie and cast her in the lead role. I had a walk-on part where I got to kiss her feet in Act Two, just before some studs got to pleasure her in time for the finale when she rode, naked, on horseback through a besieged city, liberating it, calling the shots and drawing up five year plans. She was good in that film, but she got better with every part.

I suppose she kept me up at night, but it was a benign

insomnia, pleasing to the mind, not that stinging woodfire that renders both your mind and eyes bloodshot. Like that Dylan song "Spirit on the Water." She slipped in and out of my dreams, travelling through time, holding the world to ransom with her defiant intelligence. When we spoke it was telepathically, and when I leaned over to locate the dizzying cavity between her legs, I was rapidly cast adrift in the swiftest, sweetest rapids of pleasure. No longer a languid foetus. Awaking from these dreams, I plodded around the island, rented a scooter, dispensed with a helmet, slept on the magnificent red beach, tasted the kalimari and rode a donkey whose master's face resembled an expanded sun-dried tomato. She never materialised, needless to say. She was probably stuck in the unlikeliest of places, like a dusty library, reading up on causality or candidates for the identity of Shakespeare's ghost-writer.

I discovered a nude beach and decided to sample it. There was no way that I was going to find her there, I knew that. She was the last person to go in for that kind of thing. Would utterly annihilate the mystique I felt sure she was trying to cultivate like basil. So I thought to myself: how nice it must be to swim in one's birthday suit. I tentatively stripped off layers until all that was left was a towel wrapped around my privates. Everyone else behaved with what seemed to be a total absence of self-consciousness, but I couldn't bring myself to let go, so I remained planted under an umbrella and bided my time. Finally, when I was sure no one was looking, the towel was gently removed and my full manhood revealed. Unsurprisingly perhaps, no one seemed to notice. The men strode past me confidently with their great salamis and cucumbers and black mambas and love tubes and Indian rope tricks swinging in synch with their arms; they proudly announced their wares like lorry drivers appearing at rain-splattered docks ready to have their impressive cargoes ticked off on some guy's clip board. The women were less ostentatious, but I couldn't help but stare, gawp, salivate in accordance with the usual rules of etiquette as the array of nipples, breasts, legs, black triangles of hair were paraded before me. Finally, when I had had enough of this surreally real yet numbing dose of nudity, I put something on and crept off to the beach bar and asked for a pot of Earl Grey. It was comforting to be apart from the fray and to be able to observe, rather than participate. A young woman wrapped up in a shawl looked over at me from the next table, her mermaid-blue eyes seemed to catch the sea and distil it. I glanced at her and smiled easily. She regarded me with interest and spoke in a mellifluous voice, 'I've seen you around the island. You have a red Piaggio scooter, don't you?'

I was dumbfounded but managed to hide it and summoned up some last dregs of nonchalance and levity.

'That's right. I'm impressed. You have an amazing visual memory. Do you know the number plate?'

'If I remember, it doesn't have one.'

'Absolutely right. It was a trick question.'

'You should never try and trick someone who has just remembered you when she could just as easily have consigned you to oblivion.'

'Is that a Greek proverb?'

'Not really. But in your case, the following might be more appropriate: never look a gift horse in the mouth.'

'I'm sorry, I didn't mean to do that. And you are the gift I suppose.'

'No, the gift was the fact that I remembered you. In this world today, to remember a face is saying quite a lot.'

'It's true, the world has become so crowded, so unnecessary.'

'I don't know why, but I was . . . nothing . . .'

'Please, go on, I am fascinated and very, very flattered.'

I smiled at her and I was struck by the absence of artificiality in the gesture.

'Actually, you remind me of someone, someone I once knew,' she said.

She looked away for a second. I didn't want to press her, I let her take the lead, which was what she wanted anyway, I guessed.

'He was a photographer, a war photographer, actually. You have similar hair, the way it curves up at the sides, the texture. It's hard to say why I noticed. It just struck me. I know, not the most obvious thing to notice.'

'What happened to him?'

'Don't you think it's time we were introduced, as Cary Grant says to Eva Marie Saint in *North by Northwest*.'

'I am but mad north by northwest.'

'Exactly - now let's get serious. Shakespeare's a mess, he can't do plot, he can't do endings, he can't write five decent lines of verse without making a pig's ear of everything, he is long winded, and his characters lack credibility. Why on earth, for example, doesn't Edgar reveal his identity to Lear?'

'You have a good point, I've often asked myself that same question.'

'I saw you earlier, on the beach, I saw your thing . . . '

'What?!'

'Sorry, I just wanted to say I found it sweet.'

'Are you always so forward?'

'Yes, pretty much.'
'Should I be pleased that you liked my thing?'
'That's up to you, I can't comment on that one.'
So – steadfastly refusing to give me the green light. Or maybe she had already given me the green light and I was too dumb to drive. Oh *The Sorrows of Young Burper*, I was slipping into the solar flares, crawling up to chomp me. Where was the choreographer? Where was the instruction manual? The chalk for my palms as I heaved the weights over my shoulder . . . I wasn't good at this game, this racket. Give me the dogs, the under and over dogs, I'll soon lick them into shape, but never let me get too close to women, they unravel the bandages that I've spent my whole life trying to fasten.

Maybe this one was a genius, who could say? In my time I'd been in the proximity of croc-women, busty women, bejewelled, bedecked women, but the genius woman, that was new.

'You look like you could do with a alcoholic beverage, but it must be 104 degrees in the shade, so alcohol might not be such a great idea.'
'You may be right.'
'A towel or two and I'll be an Arab, cover me with black yashmaks and turbans. I would like to disappear and they would all wonder who I was.'
'I don't follow, I'm losing the plot as usual.'
'Poor thing. Well, I mean, here, all these exhibitionists are showing off their bits, it's as if they have all painted these paintings and are trying to stick them up in a gallery, but actually the paintings are themselves and they don't quite realise that their bodies are not really independent works of art, though they would like to think they are. I'd very much

like to blow open all that vanity and walk down the catwalk, or rather the beachwalk, in shawls and masks and veils, covered and wrapped up, just to be different, but they'd bearly notice me: they might see this strange figure, half woman, half garment, hanging in the twilight, then they'd go back to their coconut juice and their pina coladas. I'd be like Peter O'Toole in *Lawrence of Arabia*, in my shawls, strutting my stuff.'

I began to think she was not only a genius but gaga as well.

'I can see from that frown that you haven't the slightest idea what I'm talking about. You might even find the sound of my voice irritating and be thinking, why doesn't she shut up now? But, you know, sometimes an eternal drone can be life-affirming. Let me give you an example. I am petrified of flying and the other day I was on one of those small planes, you know the ones with World War II propellers and no aisle space, and this woman in the seat in front of me wouldn't shut her mouth. I was already feeling kind of nervous and then we took off and pretty soon the plane was hitting turbulence. I was gripping the sides of my seat and the woman kept on chattering, and then suddenly I began to derive comfort from her voice – it was like a symbol of normality, and she was like some kind of dumb magnificent heroine. None of the plane's sickening plummeting into nothing seemed to register and I became intensely grateful for her jabbering. I thought that I should ask her for a recording of her voice so that I could listen to it whenever I'm on a plane caught in turbulence. You see it's all about contexts converging – "the mind is its own place and can make a heaven of hell, and a hell of heaven." Milton, in case you were wondering.'

'Right, well, nice talking to you, but I think I have to join all the pina coladas and exhibitionists.'

'You want to gatecrash a party with me later tonight in the village?'

I stared at her. It was a tempting offer, but I wasn't sure I could stand to be around her. Perhaps though she'd be less wired, less manic in the calm of night time. And maybe I'd get lucky; after all, this was Greece and stranger things have happened. She leaned over and pulled out a biro that was stuck in her hair and in doing so liberated the strands that had been knotted into lattices behind her ears and they fell forward beautifully, in one motion, and she jotted down an address on my forearm.

'For later, if you want to see me. It gets started around half eleven. It's by the Armeni Village Apartments, I think it should be cool. But don't go getting any funny ideas about me, ok, buster. By the way what's your name?'

'Buster.'

She smiled – and it was beautiful.

'Actually, it's Curren.'

'How interesting, you are so close to being any number of other things – currency, current, curry.'

'Yes, that kind of sums it up, I am just Curren: undefined, unrecognizable, not quite the thing I remind you of. I would like to be a curry but I am not.'

'A current bun? I would nibble on your edges. Do you want to be on top or on the bottom?'

'What?'

'My name's Amanda.'

'That's quite close to A Man.'

'But I am not, just a humble girl waiting to be swept off her feet by my Prince Alarming. I am Greek, in case you were wondering. And my real name is Efharis.'

*Island*

'Why did you say it was Amanda?'

'I'm going to go snorkelling now.'

She rose and left me with a view of her long legs, rather big-boned, but enticing in a strange way, kind of like the appeal of a stodgy meal on a cold night, a meal one might not normally relish but under the right circumstances was heaven on earth. She was right about context. It was all in the context. A Greek island, a nude beach, a crazy but brilliant girl – that was a pretty nice context I had to admit. I decided that I would go to the party – what else was I going to do? As I was mulling all this over I realised that I hadn't thought about the choreographer in a while.

2

I rolled up at around eleven. Stray dogs were prowling, scrounging for food, and lying on the steps that marked out the borders between the Armeni Village Apartments and the adjoining hotels. All around blue and white dreamy thresholds and isolated doors in their frames opened onto nothing, nothing except dizzying vistas on the crater down there, whose void had never been so beautiful and serene as the sleeping volcano promised to erupt one day and really show us the meaning of fireworks and drag us down to create another Atlantis. I sat, propped up against the steps, regarding the dogs that regarded me, that rejected, assessed, accepted me. I was thinking of the strange contrasts in life – heaven on earth, which I currently occupied and the unspeakable acts of evil that men are capable of, remembering something about how the Aztecs sacrificed people by slitting open their chests and removing their still beating hearts and displaying them in the sickest piece of theatre ever devised. And for what? To appease and please some inanimate object such as a temple. Sometimes history's bloody bucket doesn't just overflow, it positively spews out a tsunami of plasma and we are all scattered in its horror. That absolute unspeakable dread of being alive, of being part of this sad, non-negotiable thing called life which is simultaneously horrifying and amazing and that grabs you by the throat and squeezes on your windpipe until it suddenly lets go and offers you a Strawberry Daiquiri instead, which slips down easily, lubricates you, undoes the damage, offers you a glimpse of ecstasy until once more it's time for the garroting.

The party-goers were drifting into the house and there was music pulsing, a kind of mid-Atlantic thumping drum beat and some guy screaming lyrics. The crowd was a stylish one, sun-fried and weighed down with bangles, beads, sunglasses, hats, bracelets, earrings, piercings, medallions, esoteric jewels and crusted, resplendent rings which they displayed like proud parakeets. They were an affable enough lot, young Greeks, Americans, sun-worshippers, out for a bit of fun, a few tablets of illegal substances, a few hits from a joint, a few friendly penetrations and stolen kisses all under the immensity of the stars and the sky, whose sickle moon was hanging sadly as though forced to observe the party it had been denied entrance to.

I went inside; things were pretty raucous. A guitarist with dreadlocks was belting out "Voodoo Child" and its mind-bending riffs crashed and burned and we were in the incandescent zone, in the white hot marshland glowing with the dull embers of an other worldly extinction. He was playing quite near to a fish tank that a pair of identical twins had submerged their forearms into, apparently in an effort to cool off. I looked around, no one seemed to pay me much heed and I drifted, in as inoffensive manner as possible, towards the bar area and asked a barman with a magnificent Russian moustache for a Bloody Mary. He obliged me skilfully, with great good humour, smiling, as though he knew something about me that I didn't. I thanked the guy warmly and he said to me, in a thick Greek accent, 'You have good time here? Many nice people. Enjoy the night. Enjoy the beautiful island. Many many pretty girls. All for you to try. Try, my friend. Do not be shy, you ok looking guy, you want buy some marijuana from me?'

'Well, I don't know, I'm not really . . . no,' I stammered. 'Maybe. Maybe later. I should eat something first, I mean, I haven't had any dinner.'

'Ok, my friend, you go in that room, you see where there is yellow divine light, inside there they have food, souvlaki and mezedes and taramasalata. First food, then you smoke a little. Don't worry my friend, you smoke after food, make you feel fine, very good, you enjoy party more that way, I sell you best marijuana on island, 50 euro for a nice piece, you want try?'

'I think I'll take your advice and have a bite to eat first.'

'Ok, you come back, I always here, I wait for you, there is no time here on the island. No time here. Everything stays same, everything cool.'

I drifted away from him, vaguely aware of a sense that my movements were being willed by someone other than myself, that my real self had been fatally diminished. And then I saw Efharis. She was standing in the corner, dressed in immaculate white from head to toe. White head band, white sash around her waist, white scarf, white sarong, white sandals, incandescent blue eyes. She looked – amazing. Truly. The gap of time between my first sight of her on the beach and my second at this party right now seemed to straddle centuries of consciousness, great arcs of evolutionary consciousness. How was it that she was now so ravishingly alluring? What had happened in the interim? She grinned subtly when she saw me and sauntered over. She had the demeanour of someone in control. She produced a tiny flask of something and placed it to my lips and I became aware of an incredibly warm rush down my throat, fiery and electric. I was too dazzled to say anything and just stared at her and she burst into laughter. 'We were talking about Shakespeare,' she said, as though picking up the thread of our previous conversation, as though perhaps two minutes had elapsed since the Bard's name was last mentioned, and she was now busily setting the conversation back onto its groove. 'He can't do plot, he can't do endings, he can't write five decent lines of verse without making a pig's ear of everything, he is long winded, and his characters lack credibility. Isn't that so? Come closer to me. Like this, I'm having to shout.'

I did as instructed. 'Good, that's better. You look handsome. Like a man, but at the same time a little bit boyish. Like the statue of the David.' At that point I recalled a story I had read about someone called Brooks Berkenfeld who had hatched a plan to steal the David from the Academia in Florence. His cockamamy idea had been to hover above the roof in a helicopter and then to cut a hole in the roof of the Academy by means of a short pulse laser, descend on metallic wires like Batman and then, using the same laser, remove the statue from its base and yank it skywards and off to freedom.

He never actually carried out the job when he realised that he suffered from vertigo. But imagine if he had done it, imagine if someone somewhere owned the actual statue of the David. I wonder how much it would sell for? 100 million dollars? Two hundred? A billion? Could its sale pay off the American debt? No, nothing could pay off the American debt. 22 trillion dollars . . . think about it. Every ATM machine in the world combined couldn't pay off the American debt. The only thing that might do it would be a bar of gold bullion as big as Jupiter's backside or with the dimensions of George Soros' ego.

'It's nice to see you,' she went on. 'I thought about you after we met. Did you think about me?'

'Well . . . yes, I suppose so.'

'You suppose?!' She stood back abruptly and walked off like a haughty sea captain off to survey his nautical charts, and I followed her anxiously, realising, maybe too late, what a wonderful, mad, shiny jewel I may just have thrown away.

'Efharis! Please, don't walk away. I'm sorry.'

She turned and her eyes bore into me like lasers from the David heist.

'Forget it, Curren. It's ok. It's a wonderful evening. Don't you think?'

I smiled, relieved.

'But Curren, you know, there's something seriously wrong with you, you know that, don't you?'

'Yes, I do. I'm fucked in the head.'

'But it's not really you, Curren, it's society at large, it's all of us, we are all fucked in the head.'

'I guess.'

'We are living in the cesspit Curren, the sick bucket. The

Age of the Bedpan. We think the bedpan is an ice bucket and we mistake the sewers for rivers. But there's no denying it. Shit is shit is shit.'

'Are you speaking about anything in specific?'

'I am speaking about everything. Every goddamn thing. Think about it. Do you remember Richard Nixon?'

I nodded.

'When he got busted, he resigned. He sank into ignominy and notoriety. Can you imagine anything like that happening today? Can you imagine any politician resigning today? Does the concept even exist? The umbilical cords are still gooey with the bile of rhetoric and politicians' radioactive slime. Look at all these bankers – can you imagine any single one of these mother fuckers who have lied and manipulated and invented bogus statistics and bank ratings in order to ensure their pockets were lined – any of them doing the honourable thing? Committing hari-kari? My country has been bled dry by the IMF and by Germany and by the European Union. Here, on this island, life is good, but this is not the real Greece, this is an illusion. In the real Greece people are without money, without bread, my father, who is diabetic, can no longer afford to pay for his medicine. Most of my friends have not been paid their wages in one year. In Athens old people are committing suicide because they have been robbed of their pensions and their savings. And at the same time millions of dollars are being made by useless ciphers like the Royal family and Damien Worst, and all those kleftis at Goldman Sucks who ruined my country. Do you know that they created a fictitious exchange rate to shrink the country's debt? 2.8 billion euros just disappeared. But now it's appeared again, oh yes. Greece should never have entered the eurozone in the first place – it wasn't liquid enough to qualify for admittance. The Goldman bandits came up with the idea of shrinking the debt, legally and secretly. So they cooked the books so that Greece could enter the eurozone and they made a staggering amount of money from it. But if Greece had never entered in the first place, if the debt had never been hidden, we would have been a lot better off than we are now. You know mothers are being forced to abandon their babies in Greece and give them to priests and nuns? 500 euros a month is the average wage. So, my dear Curren, you see, I have a rather pessimistic view of the world at the moment. People eat shit, they watch and listen to shit and, above all, they talk shit. The average person is so stupid they probably wouldn't be able to define what stupidity means.'

I had no answer. I started to think about the choreographer again – the chances are that I had missed her finally. Life was like that. A series of moments, unrepeatable moments and you would never know what it was you had missed because it was no longer there to experience. Fortunately though there was something else to experience in its place.

Efharis moved closer to me and I felt vertigo rising, my eyes glazing over. Her beauty was all encompassing, her mind strong and defiant. She stared long and hard into my eyes. At that moment I was mesmerized, I was held by her, she was my guru, I would have agreed to anything just to please her.

'You know what would help the world, Curren?'

I held my breath, waiting for her to tell me.

'If we could somehow make the gravitational field stronger.'

'How do you mean?'

'If we could make gravity a stronger force so we wouldn't

be able to run around like fucking idiots on Chaucer's 'little spot of earth', shitting all over it.'

She smiled – it was dazzling.

'Efharis . . . I think I'm in love with your mind.' I wanted to add, 'Can I fuck it?' but I managed to stop myself. Yes, that old game of reining in, I was a master of it, tied to the masthead in the storm, while pretending to be lounging nonchalantly on a prototype beach. I was both Captain Bligh and Mister Christian, at war with myself, all because of the fresh aroma of cunt, pulling me in, making me walk the plank. Catching glimpses of the little fishes down below. Umbilical cords still gooey with the bile of rhetoric and politicians' radioactive slime . . . where had I heard that before? Had she now ransacked the contents of my mind? What was going on? Reality was melting all right, something wasn't quite right. Linear trains had been derailed and smashed as though by armies of rampaging midgets clutching little hatchets.

'I think I am in love with your mind.'

She ignored me.

'Imagine if gravity was a little stronger so we could no longer walk but had to crawl around on our hands and knees. So everyone would be forced to eat humble pie and acknowledge their absolute insignificance. It would be beautiful – it would finally bring everyone together and people would recognise their essential similarity. That's my dream, my hope.'

'Wow, that's quite an idea, how did you think of that?'

She was silent.

'Curren, how would you feel about becoming my slave?'

'Em . . . '

'I don't mean my personal slave . . . I mean my sex slave.'

'Count me in.'

She smiled and reached over and kissed me very very softly. In the prodigious blaze of Grecian sunlight I was a cloud drifting, a god upon a lotus leaf, pondering the immensity of creation, no longer burdened by the need to understand, no longer lashed by six of the best, by the whip, the imperative, the great corrugated WHY.

The party was starting to get good, it had to be said.

Then she kissed me again. This time it was a different affair. More licentious and full blooded. Like a Merlot after a nice rosé. I wasn't sure whether or not I would be tasting the Brunello later on. Or maybe the night would end with just me and a cup of camomile tea, as it so often had in the past. But she was kissing me - that was the gist of it and it was like a great Ferris wheel had been set in motion. I could feel myself falling through space. I occupied - at least for a few seconds - one small place in history's corridors of greatness and supercharged moments: life was good, so good that you knew you could never recreate it because it was lived and felt too intensely, too deeply. Pleasure is the hurricane that lays to waste all the cities and plains.

I whispered as softly as I could manage, 'Do you . . . do you feel like going back to my room? I have a nice bottle of wine. We could . . . we could . . . talk some more . . . in a quieter environment . . . it's getting a bit . . . noisy . . . in here . . . . Maybe soon they'll start throwing plates . . . like wonderful Greeks do . . . .'

'Curren . . . .' She was moving her tongue slowly around my left earlobe, ' I don't think that's such a good idea . . . you know . . . and I don't really like sex actually. I only really like kissing. This is fine by me . . . . So your butterfly collection will just have to wait . . . '

'I have no butterfly collection . . . but I do have a . . .'

She broke away from me, rather abruptly. I looked up, the guitar was screeching, the asteroids colliding and in the distance I could see couples dancing provocatively – they reminded me of snakes that had been drinking vodka. The wah wah pedal was working its wonders. It was a good party – atmospheric and transgressive. The real deal.

'Listen . . . Curren . . . I want to tell you something . . . I don't want to scare you . . . but I think . . . I need to tell you something.'

'Go ahead,' I said. In the distance I could make out a woman dressed up in a belly dancer's outfit. She had a magnificent ruby stuck in her belly button.

'The future is not a pleasant place.'

'How do you mean?'

'Something happened to me. I saw the future.'

She screwed up her eyes. For a minute it was touch and go. More and more dancers were emerging from the shadows like life-affirming cockroaches. The place was vibrating, on the point of take-off. I could hear the captain babbling something about forward thrust. G-force. Paper napkins. Please return to your seats, we are experiencing some turbulence. The turbulence is your life falling apart. Soon people would begin shooting movies, heroin, themselves.

'The future.'

'What the hell are you talking about?'

'Let's step outside for a bit of air.'

## 3

It felt remarkably peaceful after the guitar as we ambled down to the steps where five or six dogs slumbered. We took our place next to a straggly, brown specimen. The dogs might have been feigning sleep, eavesdropping on our conversation. It was as magical and as beautiful a scene as one could have wished for, the sleeping volcano down below, swallowed in a field of Prussian blue, the rows upon rows of enchanted, clean lights stretching into the distance and the gracious yawning cliffs of the island: beautiful signifiers of the past, consoling emblems of the future.

The future, she'd said.

Again it occurred to me that she was unhinged. Brilliant, erudite, well informed, but unhinged. But it was difficult to square her eloquence, her control, with insanity. She didn't display any of the classic signs of your average schizophrenic. She didn't seem jittery or paranoid, she didn't make grandiose assumptions about her own importance or speak of voices commanding her, or refer to telephones that were bugged or hidden cameras watching her every move. But she had to be a nut. She just had to be. But she was too fascinating and attractive for me to walk away.

'Last spring I spent a week in London. I had to consult some manuscripts in the British Library for my Phd, which is on Jung's theory of synchronicity. It was a wonderful spring day, and London looked very beautiful. Well, I finished up at the library and got on the tube. I remember that I was staying at a nice hotel – The Rathbone, in Fitzrovia. They have delicious, transfigured apples there, by the way. So I was on the Central line, just about to pull in to Tottenham Court Road station.

'The train arrives as usual and the doors open as usual. And I start to follow the crowds to the exit and the escalators. But then for some reason I stop. I go back to the platform and wait until the crowds have cleared. They finally all leave but then the platform starts filling up again with all the commuters and shoppers and I see that there's another train due in two minutes, going to Ealing Broadway. I walked straight down to the driver's end of the platform, right down to the edge, almost to the point at which the platform runs out and after that there's just tunnel. There's a sign telling you not to go any further. I look around to see if anyone's watching. No-one is. And then this crazy idea pops into my head. What if I were to walk through the tunnel? Actually walk to the next station? It's too frightening to contemplate. So I step back up to the platform and I wait. The train to Ealing Broadway comes and goes. I look up and see that the next train, for Hanger Lane isn't due for 14 minutes. 14 minutes. That's enough time, I think. Enough time to walk from Tottenham Court Road to Oxford Circus, the next stop. All I have to do is make sure that my legs don't touch the live rails or I will be electrocuted. So I set off. I'm so scared I think I'm going to have a heart attack. But the tunnel is well lit and actually it's relatively easy to avoid the first and third rails, which are the live ones. I walk close to the fourth, which is not electrified. As I'm walking I'm thinking that if a train comes now I will be dead as mush. But no train does come and eventually, after what seems like an eternity, I see with great relief the lights of Oxford Street station looming in the distance. I wait a second at the corner, at the point at which the tunnel stops. I spy the crowds milling about the platform. That's good, there's lots of people, no one is going to notice me. Then I slip up the little incline and make it to the platform. I'm home free. I feel absolutely amazing, flushed and on top of the world. I've just done the most radical and dangerous thing of my life. It's quite an achievement. I feel the overwhelming urge to tell someone, but I have no-one to tell. I'm so transported and dazzled and in my own world that at first I fail to notice that Oxford Street station is utterly different in appearance to Tottenham Court Road station. I don't mean that it has different colours or posters or anything like that. It has different everything. I stare at it in bewilderment. It occurs to me that the station must have been renovated recently. I go up to the walls and touch them. They have a shiny, streamlined appearance. They appear to be made of some kind of high-grade non-combustible plastic. The posters are all fairly nondescript, advertising films and so on. Then I move in a little closer to one of them and stand there, horrified. It's for a book, a novel called *The Undying* and the poster says the book will be available for instant download on people's contact lenses. That really throws me. But then it also adds 'on 13 January 2043.' I look at the text again. There's no mistaking it. I go up to another poster and look for another date. It's the same. There's some poster advertising something called Diurnal Therapy - a course aimed at people between the ages of 100 and 120 years old starting on 25 February 2043. I'm flabbergasted. It's only then that I realise how strangely dressed the other commuters are. They all appear to be wearing the same synthetic, grey suits and skirts and shoes. I turn to someone, some guy with a strange striped beard, so that he looks like a zebra, and ask him the date. He says '8 January,' and turns away. I realise how hot it is for a day in January and I am really starting to panic now. I rush along the platform and I attract a few odd stares. I can see a number of massive vending machines stuck to the wall and I stop for a second to look at their contents. The machine says it accepts 2.50, 5, 10, 20, 50 card "Vouchings." I wonder what the hell a vouching might be. I scan the choice of snacks, expecting just a few items. Instead the machine tells me it stocks sushi, curry, kebabs, wraps, burgers, pasta, pizza, fish and chips, sandwiches, soups, salads, cakes, water, coffee, wine, you name it. Plus there's a grid where you can re-charge something called your Teleroam. Next to that there's a machine selling condoms, toothbrushes, deodorant, different kinds of medication, some requiring prescriptions which have been loaded into your "Medicard", some not, and so on. Finally I come to stop in front of another poster and it just says in massive letters 'The ihome – we cut the edge.' At this point I'm freaking out completely and wonder if someone has slipped me some LSD or something. I head for the exit and instead of escalators I find rows upon rows of small steel lifts, their doors constantly snapping open and closing. I get in one of these and am surprised to find that inside there's abundant space. We shoot up and in less than a second we have arrived. The doors open and I'm amazed to find that there are no longer any ticket barriers; instead people just pass out in great droves. Oxford Street has been utterly transformed into a gigantic Los Angeles-style boulevard. The pavements have become moving walkways and there are no longer any cars. Small metallic railings run all the way up and down these walkways and everyone is clutching one of these quite happily. As they do so I am again struck by the uniformity of these people's appearance and the absence of expression in their faces. I step onto the walkway and beside me I see small panels that seem to indicate the possibility of altering the speed. I press a button and instantly the walkway swells and some pleasing, rhapsodic music starts. Next to me there's this very tiny man and I notice that some kind of transparent device has been inserted into his ear and it is flashing periodically with a red light. In his hands he is touching a very small keypad. 'Excuse me, sir, but can I ask what you're doing?' At first the man doesn't appear to understand and he struggles as though he is incapable of speech. Finally he pulls out another little keypad and types into that and his face relaxes somewhat and he manages to form words. He says, "I was just sending a thought-text." I try and hide my astonishment and hear myself say, "I'm sorry but would you mind explaining what that is?" He smiles, taps his keyboard and right there in front of me, a hologram materialises. It's a tall Indian lady dressed in a red sarong and she explains in the patient tones of someone addressing an imbecile: "A thought-text allows you to send a thought as soon as you have it to whomever you wish in accordance with POLP technology." Then she slowly gets erased and I turn back to the guy and he gives me a shy smile. We are still hurtling along in great smooth vaults and I decide to get off the walkway. As I cautiously enter one of the shops, though depository would probably be a better term, I see that there are no longer any shop assistants, just what appear to be robots, and that the till and the cashier have also been phased out. The shops are all deserted and a kind of sadness hangs over the rows and rows of shirts and sweaters and jeans. I move closer to a pair of these and reach out to touch their smooth texture. As I do so a small hologram appears next to the shelf and it says, "No workers were exploited in the manufacturing of these jeans." This strikes me as rather promising and for the first time the future appears less cold, less impersonal.

'As I'm standing then, in a state of amazement I realise that I badly need the toilet. I look around and one of these robots glides over and announces in metallic tones where I can find one. I say, "How did you know that?" It answers, "When a prospective customer's face is eloquent of enquiry or indecision we can extrapolate that they need to use the restroom otherwise known as water closet otherwise known as bathroom otherwise known as toilet." I walk away, rather disturbed by this mind-reading robot and find the place. It is marked simply FOR FEMALE ADULTS, which I assume means there is a toilet for female non-adults, or children. I go inside and everything is spotlessly clean and I enter a small cubicle. This door automatically locks itself for me and the actual toilet, which is pretty similar to the ones we have today, rises up half a meter, apparently in order to provide me with a more comfortable pissing experience. Next to the toilet there's a network of shoe-cleaning brushes, different types of toilet paper, scented, soft, moisturised, and small buttons which release air freshener into the cubicle. Then as I finish peeing, the thing flushes automatically and I grab a piece of paper to dry myself. As soon as I tug it starts feeding out automatically. Then I get up to go but before I do so a bright display switches itself on and gives me a kind of health check list. My blood pressure reading, my good and bad cholesterol levels, my blood count, the health of my heart, lungs, liver, kidneys, and recommendations for changes in lifestyle, diet, and exercise. Then a final message pops up and says that any faecal matter I might have passed will be used towards the formation of fertilizer, if I grant permission by saying yes out loud. I say that I only had a pee. The display reads, "We have acknowledged your statement and we thank you for your time." The cubicle door pops open and a metallic voice says goodbye. As I leave the shop, a hologram appears and yet another Indian woman in another sarong says, "Before you go, you might like to consider these other items which were similar to the jeans that you appeared to like earlier" and a series of goods and clothes get flashed up, but I don't stick around to see these. I stagger back onto one of the walkways and ask someone if there's any way of buying a newspaper, but he tells me that they no longer exist. The last time a newspaper was printed was in 2023. I get off the walkway and enter what appears to be a restaurant. I realise that I have no Vouchings so I have no means of paying for anything, but as I enter a small waiter robot buzzes over and seems to scrutinize me and says, "We have scanned you for available means of payment and find you to have no means of liquidity, so we are pleased to offer you a free meal, extrapolating that you must be either unemployed or homeless or penniless or all of these. Please come this way." So that makes me think that even though this new society knows everything about you and predicts your tastes and your needs, and even though it has killed off all traces of privacy and reduced everything to the level of imbecilic explanation, it has some kind of social conscience programmed into it, which is more than can be said for the society that we are in now, and it has found a way of syphoning off its surplus resources to those who need them but who can't afford to pay for them, in other words all those tons of food that we throw away every day are now being utilised and the system is learning how to apportion all that out productively. Well, at least, that was my hypothesis. The robot waiter says, "I will bring you your meal shortly," and buzzes off, and I sit at a small table which is loaded with every kind of entertainment device: a television with 5,000 channels, headphones, visual puzzles, screensavers, displays of the sky at night, the ocean, forests, deserts, underwater sea views, anything you care to mention. As I sit there, I wonder what the hell the robot waiter will bring me. I look around at all the other diners. They are all dressed in that same horrible grey material and I have the impression that conversation is rudimentary and that there isn't really much of it. It also occurs to me that even though I am in London I could be in any big city. In fact, in that sea of faces there is a predominance of Asian faces, Indian faces, Sri Lankan faces, but I don't discern any British faces. Then the robot waiter brings me a meal of beetroot and spring onions. The dessert is one small banana. And there is a cup of scalding hot green tea. Clearly this is their standard meal for the homeless: rich in potassium and iron. I take it and try my best to express gratitude to a machine. It buzzes off. Then, as I turn to look again at the diners, I notice that everywhere, all around, but displaced from the eating area, there are these little orange cubicles. In a flash it occurs to me that the handmade object, the specialised custom-made car, the specialist shop, the French bistro, the fountain pen, the newspaper, all those things that are now synonymous with individuality and excellence, have gone. My meal, similarly, is utterly bland and lacking in any personal flourish or inventiveness. It seems to me that the whole world must have turned into a gigantic shopping mall – catering with incomparable efficiency to all of our most pressing immediate physical and biological needs, but neglecting, discarding, marginalizing all that is more subtle, nebulous, dare I say it, spiritual.

'People's superficiality and shallowness had ballooned to

colossal proportions and I hadn't yet seen a single person who'd struck me as exuberant or colourful. And at the same time there seemed to have been a systematic stamping out of anti-social tendencies in people, and I had the impression that society as a whole had become more peaceful and that there were less visible signs of social unrest or injustice.

'I walk up to one of the orange cubicles and scrutinize the panel. It simply says REST POD. I guess that restaurants now incorporate beds for those who need to digest a meal or take a nap. It strikes me as a pretty good idea. Another thing that catches my eye is that a lot of the diners in the restaurant have small oval mirrors attached to bands on their left wrists. Above the mirror there's a display where alternately a green and an orange light flash. I go up to one of the diners and asked what this is for. At first he looks at me as if I am from another planet, which I suppose, in a way I am, and then asks me where I've been for the last few years. I tell him, quite earnestly, that I've been in a coma and he apologises profusely and then explains that these objects are known as Flirt-mirrors. The mirrors have some kind of software inside them that registers when someone behind or to your side is looking directly at you. The mirror alerts you to this by flashing an orange light. If that person looks at you and holds their stare for longer than five seconds the green light flashes. All of this is designed to flatter your ego or encourage you to get into conversation with your admirer. It strikes me as an ingenious idea though rather narcissistic at the same time.'

She was silent for a moment.

'Curren? Curren, are you still there?'

'Yes, I'm here, just about.'

'Well, what do you think?'

'I don't know what to think. About you. Or about anything you say.'

'Am I to infer that you don't find all this credible?'

'Well . . . actually it all makes sense . . . it all seems quite likely to happen, given the way things are going. But what I don't understand is how it was possible for you just to slip into the future.'

'Curren, I have to confess something.'

'What?'

'Just now . . . while I was talking . . . I was using you as my guinea pig . . . to see whether or not what I was saying was too far-fetched.'

'What do you mean?'

'I mean . . . for the last thirteen minutes I've been lying my head off.'

I didn't say anything. I felt humiliated, impressed, angry, all at the same time. I stood up dramatically and walked back into the party. At that moment I didn't care whether she would walk back with me or not. But she did, and I was aware of her at my side, suddenly sheepish, maybe even remorseful. She didn't say a word and I liked it that way. I was tired of her, tired of her tricks, tired of her cleverness and her inventions. Inside the party had cooled off a bit and the crowd had dwindled. The guitarist was nowhere to be seen but I could make out the belly dancer in the corner. She was talking to some guy who looked like Elvis Costello. I walked up to the bar and asked the guy with the Russian moustache for another bloody Mary. He obliged me ingratiatingly, as before. This time I noticed a new bravado about his movements that might be described as pure artistry. I was aware of Efharis standing beside me. She took my hand but didn't say a word. The barman gave me a sympathetic smile, as though he knew that I was going through a hard time because of this woman but at the same time the smile acknowledged that I had no choice but to go through a hard time with her; that I could not say goodbye to her or lose her. Efharis pulled my hand up towards her lips and kissed my palm tenderly. I was smitten by the unexpected fragility of this gesture and by her vulnerability. I stared at the bar man and he looked back at me, smiling again. This time it was a different smile. We understood each other. We spoke a language without words and it was beautiful to sample, just for a moment, the camaraderie of male bonding. The barman seemed god-like, all knowing, like he'd been in my shoes before, played the poor sea-tossed lover, been the confused misfit, suffered the pangs of love, but now had withdrawn from it all, transcended it and reached another plain of existence in which he could observe everything in quiet detachment. Glancing at those strong features I was overcome with a feeling of recognition, as though I had seen this person before, and his air of quiet finality, his complicity, was eerily familiar.

'I had to test whether or not I could get away with it.'

'Get away with what?'

'I intend to write a small book, a slim, mind-bending volume on these fictitious experiences of mine. I realise that after I finish my doctorate I can look forward to unemployment and no future. As I don't really fancy the idea of no lectureship in the world and grinding poverty, I intend to write this book and substantiate it as completely and as authoritatively as I can. Curren, have you heard of time slips?'

'No.'

'A time slips occurs when someone travels into another

time without any apparent explanation. There are numerous instances of it recorded, and usually by reliable people. I am convinced that I can pull this off and I have already been in touch with a reputable literary agent – I have every reason to believe that he is into the idea and that he believes me. I have reams of this material sketched out in my notebooks and I have already thought of ways of corroborating the evidence – photographs, voice recordings, perhaps even actual objects. I have a friend who can manufacture any kind of photographic image without revealing any of his tricks, without incriminating himself. The voice recordings – those can be synthesized with the right software. Objects, well, that's a little bit more difficult and I have to think about it, but I might be able to make use of the potentialities of 3D printers. But what the hell? Why not take advantage of people's naivety? Their stupidity? Or their romanticism? People want to be told these kind of things, that's why they all go crazy for conspiracy theories, so I'll just be pandering to that. And if I can make a lot of money by selling millions of books, all the better. The system has fucked me so who says I can't fuck the system? Curren, are you listening? What do you think? Do you want to be a part of this?'

She was a clever woman, there was no doubt about that. But could she really pull it off? Could she really persuade agents and publishers and readers that her story was true? Well, the answer was yes, she probably could. After all, people believe in all sorts of ridiculous nonsense, particularly in these threadbare days of scraping the barrel of dumb. It was just a matter of presenting it in the right way, as she said, with the right apparatus and the right credentials and all the paraphernalia of authenticity. I had believed her. I think.

I looked around me. All at once the party had re-booted itself and dense crowds had poured in and it was all go again. The streamers, the dancing on the tables, the mayhem, the never-ending soap opera of hedonism and all its myriad incarnations. Everything seemed very familiar, like I'd seen it all dozens of times before. The shirts of the partygoers. The serpentine movements of the dancers. I had been here before, I knew it. I thought - once more - of the choreographer, staging all the events, waiting backstage, watching, nodding in recognition, sleek and classy and imperturbable. Off stage and somehow all around, like an odourless vapour that you could never grasp or see. When I turned back to give Efharis my answer, I couldn't see her. She seemed to have disappeared.

It was then that I knew - without even the slightest doubt - that the choreographer would appear very soon.

# THE MOSQUE OF CÓRDOBA

CLUTCHING HIS TICKET the man walks in warily. At the instant of his entry into the mosque, for a split second, things, perception goes awry. His eyes adjust to the dim light; miraculous how the human eye can see in the muted light, his eyes see, they behold this vista that stretches out like time itself until he is swallowed in the reaches of the mosque, whose perfect arches frame and mirror more perfect arches and in the distance iron gates guard miniature chapels but it is impossible to gauge their distance and they are like chapels designed for children, for dwarfs, for insects? They seem so far away.

In the mosque he has finally reached infinity.

It seems as if he is in a gigantic hall of mirrors – what is real and what is reflection? In that place he no longer knows. He is already feeling intoxicated by the paroxysm of space, by the conjuring tricks of space. He could wonder around the mosque for eternity and never know what it was he was searching for. Perhaps he is searching for numbers, for an orientation point, for a map, for a beginning or an end. Or a candle, a light, a blessing, an absolution.

In the mosque the icons and emblems of Christianity and Islam have come together. The central nave of the Mosque is a stupendous demonstration of perspective receding into a still point, into an archway of burnished red. In the prayer room the arches funnel out in balanced volumetric compositions. The Mihrab dome above is densely woven with the most intricate patterns of adornment and figurine delicacy in a rich red velvet tapestry of stone. He thinks: here in this place Christianity and Islam seem to co-exist, here Christ and Allah might conceivably be worshipped in the same building. Could this mosque be – finally – some kind of emancipation, some kind of antidote?

He keeps walking, his reverie deepening. He wonders how he can break himself away from the mosque, how he can emerge again into the outside world, after having known such final magnificence. He brushes his fingers lightly along the lines of what looks like a column of alabaster. The smoothness and coolness amazes him. It reminds him of a crystalline shell or a displaced, gigantic tortoise, or a vertical elongated oyster. He cannot keep up with these pulsations, cannot defend himself against the arrows of beauty that keep piercing the epidermis of his mind. He wanders towards the Sacrarium chapel which is cordoned off by silky red ropes. The central panel of baroque worship seems like a protected cube that has been donated to the mosque by extra-terrestials. It sits there in a golden light, the colour of whisky. Surrounding it are altar pieces where saints and martyrs and ethereal figures float and stir and rest in contemplation. The man thinks of the column again, its smoothness, and remembers the shells of the Barricane Beach on the North Devon coast. It was there that he spent his boyhood, smoking illicit cigarettes, beckoning to friends languishing in the pallid sunlight of summer. He had been a shy boy, unsure of himself, devoting all his care and attention to his mother for whom each one of his absences from the house had meant another manifestation of anxiety as she wheezed and coughed, the victim of asbestos poisoning, which was slowly consuming her lungs. She had worked in one of the countless unsafe factories that England had been filled with in the late 1970s, before such places had been deemed unsafe. Richard had come home one evening to find his mother stooped over the living room table as she continually re-read the contents of the grubby letter she had received that morning which confirmed she was dying of Mesothelioma. Ever since that moment his childhood had been truncated and his mother had been reduced to a slight, stooped prematurely aged form and whenever Richard had been able to extricate himself from her clutches any sense of freedom had been crushed by a corresponding sense of guilt. But nonetheless it was on that Devonshire beach that he finally lost his virginity to a girl almost as shy as he was. On that transfigured coastline in the early morning light he had made love to a girl who, in his trembling and unsure arms, gave herself to him with perfect candour and they both sensed that their entry into sexual awakening was like some fabular perfection, as though the elements and nature were conspiring to make their dreams come true in a final and rare departure from the notion of nature's cosmic disinterest in man's petty little affairs. Afterwards he walked for hours along the shoreline in a state of incandescent happiness, having clean forgotten about his mother, about her constant needs, about the summer job in a solicitor's office he was shortly to be fired from, his short-term memory misting over; the dreamlike enormity of what had just happened had created a dissolving amnesia. Even the waves and the stones seemed foreign, in the whiteness of his bliss; it was as though that first coupling had lit a flame in which ordinary sensory perception was singed.

He realised that in the mosque he was re-encountering that same immersion into newness, that same sense that he was at that very moment experiencing life for the very first time.

As his admiration for the mosque deepened he was dissonantly stopped short by the wall of the world. The outer world (which he had temporarily forgotten) with all its squalor and vice, its frightful suffering and filthy commerce. He experienced a brief spasm of shock as he recalled reading about the latest atrocity committed by another Middle Eastern terror organization. What things had to happen to a man, what disfigurement had to take place for him to be willing to have his limbs scattered, for him to be willing to massacre and maim others? What false and grotesque heaven had been promised to him, had been sold to him, what continuous pounding with an anvil at the basin of his brain, eventually wrenched and disfigured and pulled apart, for him to be willing to swear everlasting allegiance to a god synonymous with evil, hatred and murder? As he was thinking about these things – the antithesis of his earlier reverie – he glimpsed a shadow that seemed to pass from behind him. He turned around, slightly nervously, to locate its source. But he was surprised to find that there was no one there. But he was sure he had seen a long shadow, long and angular and distorted, running up in advance of its owner. He glanced around him, feeling dwarfed by the enormity of the mosque's dimensions. Off in the distance he could make out a small, very gaunt figure, an old man, struggling it seemed, perhaps born down by arthritis or simply by old age. A small white handkerchief had been knotted around his head in the manner of a make-shift hat to ward off the sun. Richard imagined scenes from his life, a provincial childhood, hours of toil, perhaps in the fields, or in an office or at a school. Maybe the old man's life had been princely, or maybe it had been hell. He felt a sudden tenderness for the old man that he could not explain.

Save for the presence of Richard and the man, the mosque was apparently deserted. Richard pulled out his mobile phone and glanced at the time. He should probably start to get going soon. He wanted to catch the 3.30 train to Seville. He had booked tickets to see a flamenco show that evening. As he was studying the phone, which he had been careful to put on silent mode, he was again aware of a shadow behind him and this time it moved more slowly. He turned round to locate its source, but again he was unable to. He felt an invisible coil around his neck tighten and squeeze his larynx. He wished he had a bottle of water. In that instant it seemed as though the walls of his throat had been glued together and that nothing would part them. It was as though he were inside a subterranean cavern, being squeezed by granite structures and rocks around him, buried inside a mining shaft, comatose inside a collapsed mining shaft. He staggered towards one of the choir stalls and into a wooden chair. Everything seemed to be bathed in a greenish-grey light, everything seemed to be framed by arches and doubling lines of phosphorescent colour, as though an aurora borealis had been secreted into the mosque and was now setting its contours ablaze. He sat breathing heavily and felt his heart pound. Beyond, he could make out the central nave of the prayer room, the pillars straight and solemn.

And then, in that vacuum, that graceful cavity, some kind of vortex took form, a kind of tableaux of garish theatricality was assembled and within it Richard saw or imagined that he saw shadowy figures fighting, heaving heavy metal swords and knives and daggers and impaling one another, inhuman, diabolical figures of warfare, and far off, in the distance, he glimpsed the corpses of crucified forms, and the desecrated bodies of countless massacres, bodies heaped on bodies, pitiful, murdered humans left to rot and fall apart in a place of utter desolation, where the sun had become a blackened disc. Finally all that persisted, in this horror vision, were the outlines of skeletons and skulls on the point of crumbling into dust in the pits of a desert without name, bones piled on top of one another in devastated decay. Richard wiped his eyes, pushed and plunged his knuckles into them, and tried to banish this horror vision. He slowly ceased his motion and pulled his hands away from his eyes and opened them once more. The writhing, agonizing bodies were no longer there. This visitation from the bloody corridors of history seemed to be over. Richard sat there for a long time, feeling very shaky and weak, wondering what it was that had just happened to him. He steadied himself and opened and closed his eyes very carefully. His fears eventually began to subside. He pulled out a guidebook that he had purchased earlier and very languidly glanced through the pages until he stopped at the words:

Work began in 785, using artists from Persia, and was carried out so quickly that Abd-al-Rahman I himself was able to pray there before his death in 788.

Even the Emir, Richard reflected, needed to pray. Even the most powerful man needed to believe in something more powerful than himself.

But was violence destined to go on forever? Were the destructive forces of mankind destined never to be eradicated, never to be wiped clean, as a window is wiped free of grime? Richard was aware that his breathing was erratic and strange and laboured. Once again he wished he had a bottle of water. His mind flashed on the Devonshire beach and on Sarah's smile in the early morning sun, when the world had touched them both with its benign presence. That morning had been at once a rehearsal – unsure and hesitant – and a performance – formed and unrepeatable. Then Richard seemed to see the mythical, imagined figure of Abd-al-Rahman I rising up next to him, swelling up like a great emission of smoke from an industrial chimney, a ravaged horizon pulsing with its contaminating emissions. The Emir nodded sardonically at Richard and his smile seemed to say, "It will always be like this, servant, know that. It is what it is. There is no why. And we must follow the brutal pulse."

Richard shoved the guidebook back in his pocket and wiped his forehead, bathed in sweat. He felt some strength returning to his limbs and decided it was time to get out of there. As he began to make his way towards the exit he saw that dozens of tourists had poured in to the Mosque and were obsessively taking photographs. He could make out, hobbling towards the exit, the old man with the handkerchief. The old man looked as though he would never make it. He was grimacing in pain and exhaustion. Richard strode up to him, and speaking as softly and clearly as possible, said, "Can I help you, señor?"

The old man looked up, distracted; at first it seemed as though he didn't quite know what he was seeing, didn't realise that he was being addressed by another human being. As though he had been suddenly stopped short by the sorrowful keening of a bird; but then his moist eyes blinked a few times and Richard could see that the old man was engaged and aware again. He smiled, and Richard was astonished by how innocent, even child-like, the person standing in front of him now looked. In those instants the valleys of time that separated the two men slid away . . .

'*Muchas gracias, muchas gracias,*' the old man was mumbling as he took Richard's arm very naturally and carefully, and they both walked out together, into the blinding sunlight of Córdoba.

# CLOCK

AMY WATCHED SILENTLY as the two kittens pawed at each other, purring, playful. Or were they being aggressive? Which wasn't all that different to being playful, in the kittens' case. Why was it that, for humans, being aggressive meant dropping bombs, chopping down trees, destroying the world.

Why couldn't they just be nice to each other?

She was considering the American debt, an issue she hoped to tackle before the easier task of digesting her lunch. The sum of 22 trillion dollars was simply too gigantic to process, too overwhelming. She could just about get her head round the figure of a billion. She knew a billion was a thousand million, but after that everything went blank and the cosmos beckoned, and she could feel herself falling through it, unending blackness, sea of nothing, of void, of space twisting and backtracking on itself until space was no longer space but time barbecued and fried and disfigured.

She had seen an advert that day in *The Higham Times*.

> CHEF required at
> **Bistrot Marnie**
> Must have experience,
> and the ability to work
> in very stressful & unusual
> situations. Kitchen
> very small.

# Clock

What would it be like, she thought, if I was very small again? The times I would hide under my mother's kitchen table, trying to find my sister, who was even smaller than me. We would sit there and tape record my parents' voices as they shrieked and gossiped and attacked helpings of shepherd's pie and toad in the hole. That old-fashioned tape recorder my mum bought me, boy she regretted that. I taped every voice that crossed her threshold and when it was done she made me erase it, but I did it all again, I was too smart for her, and I kept those tapes, and every now and then I listen to my own voice, the voice of someone who was tiny and innocent and pretty and didn't know about the American debt and pesticides and the planet's implosion.

※

She applied for the job but half-way through the interview the large clock hanging on the wall fell down calamitously (as though dislodged by the tremors of an earthquake) and her would-be employer looked embarrassed and went to retrieve it. But it was beyond help and Amy was amazed to see that wads of cash had been vomited out of its body. Some kind of makeshift container had been taped behind the clock and the force of the impact had caused both it and its contents to be ejected.

'That's nothing, that's nothing', her would-be employer was muttering, scrambling around for the notes, 'it's just where we keep the petty cash, it's safer there, it's safer there, it's safer there . . .'

Amy couldn't help saying, 'That's not petty cash, that's a massive stash of fifty-pound notes.'

Mrs Haze, to cover her embarrassment, half shouted, 'The job's yours, can you start on Monday?'

Amy nodded idiotically, pleased and scared.

'Can you just give me your address and number again? I seem to have lost them.' Mrs Haze scribbled them down in large, childish handwriting and taped the scrap of paper onto her wooden desk to make sure it didn't fly away.

The kittens were pawing at each other again. Old Mrs Donatine had lost most of her marbles and was struggling to roll a cigarette at the corner of a decomposing street. Space time disintegrated before she reached the end of her task. Amy squinted at her; Mrs Donatine annoyed her, and for good reason: once two young girls on scooters had collided near the junction and Mrs Donatine had, as the elderly do, decided to monitor the situation, and something about her manner suggested she found the whole thing rather funny, something of a jolly lark. Ever since then Amy had kept her at arm's length.

Amy collapsed on her sofa and a minute later scrambled around for the business card Mrs Haze had given her. She sprang up and began searching for her pink glasses. They weren't sun glasses, they were just pink glasses, and when she viewed the world through their filters the world was more joyous, pulsating in a colourful vibration.

She wasn't sure if she could do the job; after all, the kitchen really was ridiculously tiny and very badly equipped; what kind of a bistro was it anyway? And what about all the money in the clock? Was time money? No: time concealed money and money eventually ruined time.

She opened up the billowing pages of the *Financial Times*, hoping at last to get to grips with the mysteries of the financial crisis, meltdown, recession, implosion. Greece had been bailed out, but it was going to default nonetheless; America was going to default because it wasn't prepared to give itself more money; Portugal had been bailed out, but no one wanted to bail out Italy or Cyprus because everyone in Europe was tired of helping their profligate old uncles and aunts who had told big fat porkies about what money they had in the bank. Why not just give everyone a money-printing machine and solve the problem that way? We could all have infinite wealth and not have to worry about mortgages and rent and boring jobs. Oly Mumford, her best friend, had been going steadily downhill since being fired as a toy demonstrator for accidentally electrocuting one of the kids. He had started slipping into a life of nocturnal isolation, reading every online conspiracy theory he could find, and never seeing anyone. Once when some friends had managed to prise him away for a weekend in Seville, he had stayed parked inside the hotel all day, resolutely refusing to go out in daylight hours. When they succeeded in getting him to go for an afternoon stroll, he behaved oddly, shielding himself with a boater hat, refusing to let it leave his pasty head, and coating himself in factor 60. That was when they realised he was terrified of getting a sun tan and having his unemployment benefit stopped by the Department of Health and Social Security. Poor Mumford, thought Amy. He was lost now, condemned to spend the rest of his life in a twilight zone inertia usually reserved for the elderly, for people like Mrs Donatine. But even she got out more than he did.

What would have happened if Mumford hadn't lost his job? What would have happened if Amy hadn't found her job today? If the clock hadn't fallen and revealed its treasure trove of cash . . .

The doorbell rang, more aggressively than usual, it seemed to Amy. She took off her pink glasses and opened the door. A tall, official looking man was standing outside.

'Miss Cauldron?'

'Yes.'

'Amy Cauldron?'

'Yes.'

'I'm sorry to bother you, Miss Cauldron. My name is Adonis Herriman of New Scotland Yard.'

He flashed a badge and Amy wondered whether she had somehow become, without her consent, an extra in a movie.

'I'd like to ask you a few questions about your would-be employer, Mrs Haze. Your address was stapled and nailed to her desk. We raided her premises earlier this evening.'

'Gosh. Really?'

'Yes. It seems that Mrs Haze was using her restaurant in order to lure customers into the back room where unsavoury practices took place. She also had quite a lucrative money laundering practice. She was smuggling diamonds in tubes of toothpaste from Switzerland and pawning the diamonds in London. The restaurant was just a cover you see.'

Now Amy understood why the kitchen was so poky and poorly equipped.

'I see,' she said with judicious calm.

'Did you notice anything strange about Mrs Haze when you met her?'

'Not really, but her clock was stuffed full of cash, which struck me as a bit odd, but you know, I don't like to judge people's habits that much. Well, after all, people are free to do with their money as they like.'

There was a pause.

'Did Mrs Haze say anything during the interview?'
'Anything?'
'Anything that stuck you as odd? As revealing?'
'She did say one thing, I suppose.'
'Yes?'
'She said, "Some of the customers like to pinch the waitresses' bottoms, but don't think anything of it. It's all good fun."'
'I see. Thank you.'
'Inspector, does this mean that the bistro is closed now?'
'Yes.'
'So I won't be working there after all?'
'No, you won't. Thank you for your co-operation, Miss Cauldron.'

He walked off with an incurable air of sadness. She slid her glasses back on.

Pink.

But this time it didn't quite work somehow.

A strange eerie sensation sprang up, out of nowhere. She wondered what kind of unsavoury practices had gone on at the back of the restaurant . . . Maybe something to do with the occult? Like that scene in *Eyes Wide Shut?* The evening swelled with ghosts and disembodied, trapped voices struggling to claw out of the prison of the intangible. Amy sensed them calling to her, trying to pull her into an unknowable and seductive void.

She shut the door and scrambled around for her ancient tape recorder and the old cassette of her voice when she was tiny, when she was innocent and could fit under tables. She pressed PLAY and heard herself singing, with an exquisite mixture of confidence and hesitation, that quality that only children have, which turns even mistakes into miniature icons of grace, '*Row row row your boat gently down the stream. Merrily, merrily, merrily, merrily, life is but a dream.*'

Then it was no more, this relic, this sweetness, this fragment made of gossamer shadows. Amy felt sad, then she felt numb. Her eye fell on the front page of the *Financial Times*. The headline said

CLOCK TICKING FOR AMERICA

# THE CHIMERA

The immaculately groomed man is walking rapidly, precisely. If he is in a hurry it is hard to imagine that it is because he is late or because he has miscalculated, or misjudged the length of time it requires him to cross the colossal square. If he is in a hurry it is because he wants to be in a hurry, because he enjoys being in a hurry.

The square is so vast that the human eye cannot take all of it in. A camera with the widest angle lens in the world would capture only one tiny fragment of its enormity. The only way to see the square in its entirety would be to view it from above, from an aeroplane, but then the impact of its size would inevitably be diminished. He is a tiny speck in the square, a black figure slowly moving across a hard landscape of metal and high-rise tower and office blocks that loom around the edges of the square like the component parts of a super computer that is running the world, and has been running the world for millennia. The men who designed the super computer have long since died and their ashes have been scattered or their corpses have disintegrated, but they designed this thing and now it reigns supreme and no one knows anymore how to switch it off and its tentacles are stuck in everything.

He stops and tightens his grip on his sleek suitcase; it feels smooth and luxurious. As he does so he looks up at the sun, which is attaining its maximum glare and heat. The whole of the square is doused in its sulphurous haze. For a moment the man is dazzled, stupefied by its power, and the buildings and office blocks (which all appear to be deserted) give off blinding reflections as the streamlined windows turn into solar panels and mirrors. He is cradling his face, shielding his eyes. There is not one living soul in that translucent furnace of modernity who can offer him comfort, assist him. He drops to his knees, the suitcase comes to rest beside him like a great block of concrete.

Inside the high-rise building, the escalators continue to roll, monotonous signifiers of the mechanistic universe. The reception area is deserted, the massive glass windows are so clean as to be virtually indiscernible. No one comes, no one goes. An atmosphere of overwhelmingly antiseptic cleanliness permeates everything – a stain, a blemish, a leak, would be magnified, would appear catastrophic. There is a humming sound and a metallic click. The reception area suddenly seems alive, active and red lights on a panel flash on, one by one, in a visual symphony, a cold symphony of meaningless patterns. The lights grow more frenetic and flash like strobes in a discotheque. From beneath the surface of the reception area, a monitor slowly starts to ascend. It is about two metres across and its screen projects images of the entire building, its interior, its exterior, its bathrooms, offices, garages, corridors, desks, lockers, filing cabinets, water coolers, conference rooms, cafeterias, all silent, all empty, all bereft of humanity, of even the faintest suggestion of a human presence, of a human consciousness or sensibility. The images flicker in grainy black and white, replaying, flashing, cross-cutting with one another on the giant screen. It is like a video installation, like a fragmented film divided into fifteen hundred separate images that run simultaneously. Then the images appear in high definition, in colour, and the whole paean to emptiness begins again; it is magnificently hollow, the long, sterile corridors, the bodiless elevators, the florescent lighting to illuminate a building that consumes as much power as a small city.

She sees him from afar and wonders if she may have seen him before, in some other place, in a far off context, in a dream. She tries to understand if she has caught him at the dying moments of a race, has he come in at the finishing line, on the point of expiry, or at the earliest moments of a birth, when life is still too new to be tasted, to be understood, but he is like an aged foetus, staggering in the noon sun. She has a powerful telescope on a tripod aimed at his face and can discern each line, each crease, each pimple, each spot on his face. From where she sits or stands or waits or reclines, his face is alien and there is no meaning in it, there is no meaning in it, she cannot fathom what a human face means, she stares through the powerful lens, she points the telescope towards his torso and zooms in on his suit, its smooth cut, the exceptionally silky surface.

He is supine, as though he has been slaughtered in battle. The suitcase is beside him, there is nothing, no one around. He can hear his own heartbeat, it is pounding with insane force, he has the impression it is about to vault out of his chest. All around the buildings move in closer. He pulls the suitcase towards him and glances at the enigmatic facades, the impenetrable spaces of this immensity, this meaningless matrix designed to give the impression of efficiency, of order, of control. He pulls the suitcase closer still. He flicks the case open and stares at the contents, exhausted.

※

She moves the telescope closer to his face and zooms in on his features, his blue eyes, his tanned skin. She punches some buttons on a remote-control and an image flashes up on the wall directly opposite her. It is of the same man lying down there, on the square, prostrate and exhausted. She punches some more buttons. The image gets slightly clearer, slightly larger. There he is, caught in a projection on the wall, in his suit: a photograph that has suddenly materialised from nowhere. She pushes the telescope to one side and lightly touches some keys. On the wall the man is naked now. His body is pristine and tanned and trim. His stomach is rigorously defined, hairless, his chest is rugged and his legs are elegant and magnificent. The man's penis is flaccid and rests in a nest of black pubic hair. She continues touching the keys. The pubic hair suddenly assumes a heart shape and changes colour. Now it is pinkish red. The penis, still flaccid, grows slightly wider and thicker. A few spots appear near the pubic hair and a tattoo of a butterfly takes shape near the man's shoulder. His face darkens slightly and three days of stubble appear. She stares at the image, pleased by her creation. Her hand reaches languidly for another remote control panel and she presses some buttons on it. The chair that she is sitting in suddenly reclines and she moves to unbutton her trousers and reaches for the opening of her underwear. She slides her fingers inside and starts to move them. She presses more buttons and the man's penis starts to grow and become erect.

*The Chimera*

She watches it as it rises and swells and her movements grow wilder and more savage. She presses more buttons and the man's penis is now fully erect. She is close to orgasm.

He lifted himself from the ground and closed the case. The sun was less virulent, less oppressive. He dusted himself off, though there was no dust. He looked leaner, more emaciated. He looked like a billioniare heroine addict. He started walking towards the office block, his tiny figure engulfed in the shadows that emerged from all around like fragments of voids seeking to re-form and become one. The wind was getting up and he was grateful for it. For the balm it offered and the hint of animation in an otherwise stultifying universe. He was finally nearing the office block; as he came within five metres of the sliding doors, his image was photographed a thousand times and was instantly relayed back to the monitor and the screen that continued to play its silent, mind-numbing images. He looked at the bold letters inscribed outside with arrogant certainty: LENTOMAN. He walked through the door and announced his name. A metallic voice that seemed to issue out of nowhere acknowledged him and granted him permission to enter the building. He touched a panel that activated an elevator, which swiftly rode downwards and its doors snapped open. He stepped inside. As he did so, a panel fell open, and a scalding cup of coffee was poured and offered to him on a silver platter. Sterile music played and a television screen displayed statistics from the stock market, from various stocks and shares websites, from information outlets. The ride was swift and he took one very quick sip of his coffee before discarding it in a small opening next to the door. He stepped out, still grasping his suitcase tightly.

The floor, the 235th floor, to be precise, was deserted, as was the entire building. He was the only person in the building. He walked close to the long, streamlined window that seemed to run to infinity, and felt a strong wave of vertigo pass through him as he peered down into the void of the square.

The whole office block was run by computers, every aspect of the building's activity was overseen, supervised, and executed by computers. And in that spotless immensity, a vast electronic trading facility existed, numberless rows of computer servers. These computers were robot traders – they had been programmed by other computers that had been, at some time in the past, programmed by humans. The robot traders made their own decisions about when to buy and sell – they had autonomy. These were algorithm traders, identifying fleeting discrepancies between the available market prices and what an acceptable, alternative market price might be – as postulated by the computer. In these discrepancies, the colossal potentialities of computer trading were born, as the tiniest of profit margins, duly monitored across innumerable instances of buying and selling and countless transactions, eventually and cumulatively yielded unthinkable sums of money.

The computers had also been programmed to oversee and execute every communication, to write every email, to make and take every phone call, to calculate every financial computation, to devise every budget plan, to dream up every marketing device, to concoct every press release – it was all done by computers. It had been agreed by LENTOMAN's board of directors that, in the interests of public relations and an attractive image, the whole vast office block should continue to be lit, to be operated, to exist in order to create the illusion of a functioning, human outfit housed in a functioning, human environment, when in fact all the work that went on in there could just as easily have gone on in a gigantic underground bunker. The building itself was a façade. A chimera.

The woman reached for some tissues and wiped herself. She reached over and pressed some buttons. The image of the naked man was at once erased. She rolled the telescope over to her, still breathing erratically and rapidly. She peered into the telescope – the man was no longer there. She searched all over the square for him but found no trace of him.

The man walked towards the first office he could find. He yanked open the door and sat down, pulling out a handkerchief and wiped his brow carefully. He opened his suitcase. Inside were some locks of hair, delicate, luxuriant, real human hair. He curled and uncurled them in his hands and savoured their soft, pleasing texture. For a moment he felt tranquil and his agitation seemed to have fled. The sun was less oppressive and the horizon of metallic forms less jagged and dissonant and hostile as he stared out at that chain of interlocking grids.

LENTOMAN had been brought to bankruptcy when a computer algorithm malfunctioned. The computer bombarded equity exchanges with orders to buy billions of dollars' worth of shares in crude oil. The shares dipped in price by thirteen percent two days later, when there was a gargantuan oil spill in the Atlantic Ocean. Approximately sixty-thousand barrels of oil were leaked in less than twelve hours. The malfunctioning computer then actioned the wholesale selling of the shares, thus racking up about $800 million worth of losses. LENTOMAN's equity price was erased by ninety-five percent and the company was brought to its knees. LENTOMAN had been forced to file for bankruptcy – and the receivers had been called in. There was no way out. The chairman knew this. He yanked open a window and slipped through it, into the void below, tumbling down the length of two hundred floors and dying of shock long before his impact with the sun-cooked ground.

Through her telescope she saw his body, contorted on the ground. She couldn't connect with what she saw – it was as removed, as meaningless, as the images she created on a daily basis, that she manufactured and chased. He wasn't real, she repeated to herself soporifically, none of it was real: his walk through the square, his fall, his death, none of it. No more real than a dream. No more real than fiction.

LENTOMAN said the sign, with blazing certainty. But LENTOMAN was no more, it had already passed into the abstraction of history. The cold landscape of numbers, of non-negotiable calculations, had sealed its fate.

Tomorrow she would devise and play another game.

# THE RICH AND THE SLAUGHTERED

'I'LL TELL YOU a story that contains the secret of the world,' said the Professor. His eyes were intense and more piercing than usual, as though he had inserted drops into them to make them glow more brilliantly. He seemed to have acquired the bearing of a feted theatrical actor, entering into a parallel existence: more defined, more memorable, more crystalline. His hand reached for the glass of brandy that his companion had poured for him while they sat in leather armchairs and viewed the familiar scene before them in the comfort of the Royal Automobile Club, in the company of bankers and barristers and retired colonels.

'I was thinking of a dinner I once attended; a very elaborate affair, it should be said. It was rather like a game, like a game of chess. This was in the late 90's and dignitaries, ambassadors, diplomats and some stray representatives of royalty were in attendance. Seated next to me at a table for thirty people was a rather distinguished-looking man. I later came to understand that his name was Joseph Deedes. He was a war correspondent and leaned to the left. He had covered some of the worst atrocities of the twentieth century: Rwanda, the Bosnian war, and the first Gulf War. He was telling the guests some story about the waiters in a five-star hotel in India somewhere, all dressed in white and moving about elegantly like swans. They had, he remarked, an air of troubling subservience. He said, in a clipped, impeccable accent, "I was aware of this residual sense of insolence emitting from the British residents of the hotel, who still felt it was their divine right to behave rudely towards the too deferential waiters, who still seemed, to me at least, to be trapped in servile inferiority, a remnant (I imagine) from years of suppression and ill treatment. Of course, this made perfect sense because when people have been browbeaten and kicked in the teeth and made to beg and plead, it would be only natural that they wouldn't be able to put aside old patterns of survivalist behaviour." I looked at Deedes searchingly. He must have known that this was precisely the kind of place – with its formalised setting, its illustrious guests, its aura of privilege and affluence – where such observations might not go down too well. He winked at me, because he could see that I, much like himself, didn't really belong there. We were both playing a part, I suppose, but he played it better than I did. He was a kind of Lawrence of Arabia figure, dashing and elegant, and he knew that England, and all its slightly ridiculous laws and unwritten rules, did not really represent his essential self, which was nomadic and wild. Deedes really thrived when embracing travel, the open road, and unadulterated chaos. So we shared a certain kind of sense that the evening was farcical, grotesque even, with all these bejewelled ladies and affected people raising their glasses and helping themselves to champagne, the price of a single bottle of which could probably have fed a family in Somalia for three or four years.

'I could see that Deedes' comments were rocking the boat: a pale, silent man was beginning to look uncomfortable. Sensing this, Deedes pulled back and said, very pleasantly, "This pheasant is outstandingly good, is it not?" The comment seemed to be indicating that all was as it should be once again and that the skeleton of social injustice had been shoved back once more where it belonged – in the cupboard marked Irrelevant. Our hostess – her name was Lady Rathmere – had a remarkable set of operatic breasts that palpitated under her Rococo dress like buoys heaving on a tempestuous sea – she turned to Deedes and said, breezily, "Mr Deedes was always a fan of the underdog, but he could never quite bring himself to admit that his wages were paid by those who ensured the underdog stayed in his place." Deedes took it all in his stride and lifted his glass, knowing that the best way to irritate this monster was by not rising to the bait. He said graciously, "Ah, the wages of honest labour." This seemed to rattle Lady Rathmere a great deal. An elderly waiter, who happened to be passing as he re-filled the wine glasses, was berated by Lady Rathmere as a result, and she took him to task for failing to have allowed the wine sufficient time to breathe. For a full three minutes she viciously bullied the poor old browbeaten man for his breech of etiquette, for failing to do justice to the bottle of, I think, Mouton Rothschild. She made it clear that if he were to make another mistake along those lines he would be out on his ear and that the world was filled with people who would be able to replace him at the drop of a hat. She implied that this particular bottle of wine cost the equivalent of a month's salary and that his lack of ability had effectively ruined the experience for all concerned. The old man stood there, looking shocked and sick and began to perspire. He managed to mutter a few words, and then she sent him on his way. It was a sickening display of the very kind of behaviour Deedes had been talking about, that primordial arrogance that marks those who hold positions of power. Deedes looked thoroughly disgusted and bit his lip. One could tell that he was on the verge of a verbal explosion the like of which had never been seen before, but he contained himself. I could feel his body tense in fury and anger as he sat there, trying to assimilate what had just happened. Then, with perfect equanimity, Deedes rose to his feet and the whole party suddenly fell silent. Knowing that he was about to lose favour with this circle of highly influential people, knowing that he was about to seriously injure his reputation, and possibly be abandoned to the cold winds of exile, he nonetheless did something that marked him out as a man of greatness and integrity. "Madam, you will forgive me, I hope, for leaving this cheerful party, but having witnessed the coarseness of which you are capable I find myself too nauseated to breathe the same air as you or to remain seated at the same table." It was one of the most electrifying moments I have ever witnessed as the stunned faces all locked eyes with this man declaring his solidarity with the waiter, daring to speak up when the majority of mankind would have kept its mouth shut. I was so stirred that I too rose, driven by an impulse of loyalty. For once in my sorry existence I would do the right thing, no longer keep my opinions to myself, and act in accordance with decency. I said a few words about how I felt I also had to take my leave and wished to stand alongside Mr Deedes. We left the place as quickly as possible. I felt euphoric and Deedes glanced at me with unmistakable admiration and affection. We didn't say an awful lot, I suppose there wasn't that much to say. We walked in silence for a while and I monitored him: he looked agitated, as though realising the cost of his probity, and a cloud seemed to hang over him. We got into a black cab and Deedes suggested that we stop off at his club, this very same club we are now seated in. He seemed to calm down as he sipped on a single malt and lit a fat cigar. Somehow we felt at ease in each other's company, though we barely knew one another. Our act of mutiny bound us and it was miraculous to see the premature intimacy that it created. I didn't want to press him because I knew that he was the kind of man who would only speak when he felt the urge to, and to pin him down with childish questions would more than likely irritate him and make him clam up altogether. As he smoked his cigar he looked up in a forthright manner and began, "You know," he said, "as that old battle axe was hauling that waiter over the coals, a sudden memory flashed into my brain. Years back I was posted in Baghdad, this was during the first Gulf War. The Americans has just started their first tour and the city was already decimated. The night sky was filled with incandescent light that you might think signalled celebration or joy, until you stepped back and realised that it was the harbinger of annihilation and death. The vaporizing and unremitting destruction of modern warfare, which once witnessed can never be erased. It incinerates the membrane of your mind. No one in their wildest nightmares can conceive of the horror of war and the agony, the clinging, unceasing agony it imparts on defenceless civilians. The next morning as I surveyed the absolute ruin, I came across an Iraqi boy. He couldn't have been more than five. He had had his legs blown off. He was still breathing but that was a terrible realisation, because I knew he would have to regain consciousness into a life with half of his anatomy cut away. It was . . . there are no words. It was pitiful, so awful that even now I feel a shock that renders the world senseless. I lifted the child in my arms and found that my eyes were streaming with tears that I hadn't shed since boyhood. There I was holding this poor maimed body, scrambling around, madly wondering if I might be able to locate his severed limbs; I had an idea that it might be possible to re-attach them, but I eventually had to accept that they were lost in the debris and ruins. There I was, in hell, the absolute living hell that men have created for their fellow men. At last I managed to get the child to a hospital; my team and I drove him in a Jeep to the nearest medical unit we could find. On the way there he regained consciousness and I can still hear his screams of agony. Needless to say, the unit was rudimentary and barely functional, zero hygiene observance, barely any medical supplies, but they had morphine, thank God, they had morphine and they injected him immediately with it. I stood there, watching, weeping. This was the memory that flashed through my mind when Lady Rathmere began scolding the waiter, telling him off for not giving the wine enough time to breathe. What pettiness, what indulgence. And I thought to myself, here we are seated amidst absurd levels of comfort and luxury with exquisite food and drink, absolute decadence and abundance, and there, at the polar opposite, in scattered places throughout the world, a dark, dismal hell exists, stripped of everything that makes life worth living. That is life, I thought: at once the beautiful garden of the rich and the cold abyss of the slaughtered. What a pathetic mess we have made for ourselves, what a blood-soaked mess is life. It's all so unnecessary, so utterly unnecessary."

'I stared at him, moved and dumbfounded. After a minute's silence I asked him for a cigar and he offered me one, with that irresistible charm that he could summon at will. I cut the end off and he passed me a box of matches. It was good for me to focus on something, to light the match and hear it fizz and burn, to get the cigar to smoulder, to take my mind off the harrowing things that he had just told me. Then we smoked together in silence for a moment. There was nothing else left to do.'

# THE MELTDOWN

SOME YEARS AGO, a diabolical fire, triggered by lightning, ravaged Donmark cathedral. It was a terrible tragedy, though fortunately no lives were lost and no one was injured. However, most of the cathedral was burnt beyond repair. The Donmark City Council, in conjunction with the Diocese of Y-, decided that an altogether new building should be designed and erected in place of the old. So they approached the celebrated architect, Grimsdale Rollo, who proposed an audacious idea: a small-scale imitation-Norman cathedral made from concrete and limestone, with stained-glass windows, and an external, protected, gigantic pipe organ.

Five years later, the project had been realised, and everyone was happy. Rollo walked off with a considerable sum of money, the city council congratulated itself on its daring and good taste and the local press gushed over this symbol of cutting-edge architectural modernity. Countless tourists flooded in to the quaint little city, greedily taking photos of the cathedral and its pipe organ with their digital cameras.

Whilst staring at it, however, most of the locals felt a little uneasy. It was certainly bizarre. The whole thing was an outlandish hybrid of stone and pipes and brass and valves.

The colossal central thrust of interlocking, curved tubing pointed towards the heavens. It was as though this ersatz Norman austerity had been finished off with an after-thought: the addition - or rather superimposition - on its spires and columns of this massive apparatus of musicality. What was normally housed inside a cathedral now provided the exterior with a second, displaced skin. The sound that the organ produced, when all the stops were out, would have been deafening, smiting the listener with all of its armour-plated force. Consequently, the thing was never actually played as Donmark, with its quaint shops and tearooms, would have been laid waste by the aural equivalent of an atom bomb. The whole thing was protected from the elements by an immense, raised shield that stood atop the highest towers of pipes like a fragmented, ossified tent.

The village schoolmaster, Mr Luces, was an amateur organist and he was particularly fond of the organ works of Ferruccio-Valentin Clemente, an obscure nineteenth century Italian-French composer. Clemente had been a child prodigy, and once, according to legend, had astonished Paginnini after a recital in Parma, playing Paginini's 24th caprice on the piano while blindfolded. Clemente became a kind of performing monkey for a while, pushed zealously by his baker father, who cared very little about music and a great deal about money, insisting the boy do endless rounds of concert tours in Europe and Sicily. Eventually Clemente gave it all up at the age of nineteen and shifted his attention to composition. The illustrious music critic Eduard Hanslick once passed judgement on one of his quartets and it is worth quoting his remarks in full just to get an idea of the violence of the great critic's reaction:

'Ferrucio-Valentin Clemente's music puts one in mind, principally, of the Black Death. When one hears it a violent nausea takes hold. Mercifully, once away from the presence of this music, life returns and so does sanity. Clemente has shown us that, with the best will in the world, certain individuals, no matter how hard they try, can only produce works that are, at best, sickeningly bad, and at worst, incontestably evil. With this in mind I would urge Clemente to take his own life and spare the world, which is already replete with ugliness and horror, from having to stomach any more of his abominations.'

Clemente, perhaps understandably, never recovered from this blow.

His life was to take ever darker turns. His first wife threw his musical scores in the Seine after she found out he was having an affair with her mother, and for good measure decided to set fire to his Pleyel piano. The fire engulfed the whole house, which Clemente happened to be inside. He escaped with his life, but he was never able to play another musical instrument again. He went into isolation, now a hobbling cripple, and devoted himself exclusively to composition, one of his special innovations being the invention of a diatonic scale that prefigured Wagner's chromaticism by two decades. Clemente moved to the picturesque town of Taormina and eventually died of syphilis there, thought to have been caught from a prostitute during his student days in Freiburg.

It was possible that Mr Luces, in some way, identified with Clemente. He too was a troubled man and, whilst he enjoyed relative affluence and had friends and admirers, life in a second-rate grammar school did not really satisfy his deepest needs. Some months earlier he had decided that, in order to give his life more meaning, he would become a human-rights activist. He had been particularly moved by the plight of

Pakastani women whose faces had been hideously disfigured by acid thrown on them by insane or jealous husbands, often their only crime being their beauty, which the men resented. Mr Luces spent half a year interviewing hundreds of women in Pakistan, all of them scarred, scorched shells of their former selves, their faces ravaged, having the appearance and texture of hideous immovable masks. He had started a movement on the internet to make their plight more well known, demanding justice for them. But justice was rarely accorded and many of the women ended up taking their own lives. After his name became quite well known and his efforts were applauded, Mr Luces began to receive all manner of emails and letters showcasing the stupidity, vice, ignorance, prejudice and insanity of the world and people, taking him to task for the following: failing to understand Pakastani culture and presuming to interfere in it as a foreigner; protecting women who were essentially whores; simplifying things and misrepresenting them; being an arrogant and ill-informed Westerner; sticking his nose into things that didn't concern him; and trying to turn wives against their loving husbands. The most demented and unbelievable emails of all were from women who felt sorry for the men who had thrown the acid on their wives' faces, as they went on about how these men were misunderstood, sensitive souls who were in pain.

Mr Luces had a complete mental collapse when he realised the true extent of humanity's hypocrisy, cowardice and misogyny. He felt betrayed and violated for having tried to do good, for having tried to help these women and stop these attacks and for trying to bring these barbaric men to justice. Instead of being thanked, the world and all its sticky little minions and brainwashed pygmies and fools and fascists were raging at him and collecting at his doorway like maggots in rivers of blood. Instead of being thanked for trying to scrape the shit off the world, everyone was telling him to leave that shit intact and not to touch it because he had no right to. Instead of being given a medal, which he thought he deserved for finally doing something good and right and noble, he was splattered in buckets of filth and slandered and vilified by foul-mouthed, vindictive cowards. He lost all love for humanity at that point and he concluded that people could never be saved, could never be cured or healed, and that the world was destined to go on marching in darkness; a mad, demented death march ruled by the iron rhythms of cruelty and barbarism, striking out its metallic beat for time immemorial. He managed to make it to the Accident and Emergency unit of the nearest hospital and collapsed in exhaustion and hysteria. They gave him Lexotan and Penbutolol and Setraline and Xanax and he slept for three days straight.

It was three in the morning. The sickle moon was hanging in silvery beauty, and the town was asleep – perhaps it had always been asleep. Overhead the sky was inky black; it was so black that dawn seemed inconceivable. Mr Luces was sitting, peering out of his bay window, clutching a nearly expired cigarette, considering what lay before him. His small house looked out on a scene of idyllic beauty, the green common glowing in the moonlight, its daffodils just now coming into bloom; beyond there was the castle and the tidy array of shops, tearooms, pubs; all civilised signifiers of a cosy, safe, middle-class life, duly rendered antiseptic and germ-free. He considered the life of the town – its gentility, its shrouded citizens who were all bound by strict social conventions, and glimpsed only grey, shrouded horizons. Would Fred Klems, the local postman, Mr. Luces wondered, ever witness the sight of a meditating yogi in Kerala? Would he ever know the beauty of the setting sun in Provence? Would Alice, the curvaceous barmaid of The Cock and Bottle, ever realise that the English tabloid press had cynically devised a seductive trap that ensnared people, made them desperately seek for a fame or a glamour that would never come? Would Marjorie Bowles, the local pharmacist, one day realise that life was not merely waking and working and supper and television, that another music played somewhere, there was another view somewhere, where the flowers were sweeter, the breezes warmer, where toil and hardship were not the only features of an etiolated, faded landscape? Would she ever listen to Ferrucio-Valentin Clemente's organ music and have her brain re-configured by its terrifying pulsations? Tonight she would. Tonight she would. Tonight was the night. He had decided. Mr Luces had had it all planned for months now.

Being on friendly terms with the head porter of the cathedral, Mr Luces had asked him if he could take a look at the principal key to the cathedral, a long, corrugated affair, which the porter had been only too happy to show him. While the latter's back was turned, Mr Luces pressed the key into a square of soft clay housed in a little tin box, so that its shape and teeth were clearly outlined, thus giving him an excellent record of the key's exact dimensions and shape. He snapped the tin box shut and slid it into his pocket and returned the key to the porter with some words of admiration. He then had a copy of the key made from this clay outline. And now he pulled that copy out of his jacket pocket, stubbed out his cigarette, and began to walk towards the cathedral, where a little light glowed in the distance, and he felt like he was out alone on a little fishing boat in a giant ocean, perhaps shortly to be buffeted by winds and torrential rain, perhaps shortly to capsize.

He opened the door of the cathedral noiselessly and flashed his torch until he found the organ console. It felt eerily quiet at that hour and for a moment he had the impression that he was being watched by a shadowy figure in a cassock. But he knew that he must have been mistaken. His fingers felt for the studs and stops lovingly and carefully. This was it, this was the moment of complete and utter beauty. He began to play: Ferrucio-Valentin Clemente's *Toccato in B Minor*.

At once, landing like a thunderbolt on the sleeping town, came this sound, which wasn't even really a sound, more of a force, a power, a damnation, smashing into their sleep and dreams and rendering them awake and terrified. The Grand Guignol of the music announced itself, the swelling scales and ascents rose up like Venetian masks, rising from the depths and multiplying as the whole of existence became a kind of demented carnival of uncanny vibrations. The music blew and swayed like a great calamitous gale, as the force of the sound caused branches to shake and doors to rattle, as if an earthquake was holding the world to ransom. Terror stalked the music, naked Gothic terror, and Clemente's harmonies and chords and progressions, at that insane magnitude of volume, seemed to offer up a final Biblical revelation, a canvas within which scenes of disaster unfolded; as if the score to the History of the World's Madness had just been composed and was at that instant being given its premiere. Mr Luces's ears were bleeding, but he was delirious with joy, with mad, uncontainable joy, and he swayed from side to side as his fingers raced across the stops, and the pedals below him rose and fell. He was smiling, he was laughing hysterically through his tears, frantic, self-cannibalising laughter, he felt his whole body convulsed in one luminous orgasmic onslaught of the senses. He had fused with the music as completely as two lovers grinding their limbs against one another.

People were rising, scrambling around for their clothes, trying to block out the sound with ear plugs, hastily grabbing their bath gowns, trying to understand what was going on. How had anyone managed to get inside the cathedral? Which madman was it? Would it not stop? Would it never end? The heavy vestiges of sleep bore down on them, though the music was thrusting them skywards, urging them to throw off their shackles and look upon the stars. The struggle, the dissonance was too great and this nocturnal eruption of terror and sound, this unrelenting dark grandeur was rejected in disgust and people cursed and raged and fumed as they tried to push the music to the sides of their lives. They hated that vile sound, they were determined to put a stop to it, grind it underfoot and spit it out like a plum stone, like the pip of a grape. They began to get dressed and poured out into the streets, all in one motion, all with one accord, aimed for the cathedral where they would finally seize upon the lone lunatic who dared to rob them of their precious sleep. They would teach him a lesson he would never forget, they would crucify him.

They would castrate the little anarchist.

Mr Luces went on playing. He knew the end was fast approaching, but he could not stop, he just couldn't and he was in a place far, far away from pain and disappointment. Soon he would be afforded a view of the meadows, soon his face would be irradiated by a special light: Ferrucio-Valentin would appear and they would talk, of music, of beauty, of the consolations of art, and their talk would go on long into the night, which was no longer night. He went on playing, laughing, weeping salty tears, waiting for the end.

# THE BALLS

I WAS GOING to tell you about this guy Salvatore, a fruit and vegetable seller in Florence with a raging temper. He was not a man you would want to cross. He was fifty years old, had tattoos all over his body, two false teeth and most of his hair and a limp, the kind of limp that might have resulted from a motorbike crash, or from a clash with another person as nuts as he was. Actually, he walked like that because he had polio as a child, though he never referred to it, believing that if he did it would bring bad luck, so he touched his balls, as Florentines did, to ward off evil, whenever evil seemed about to come his way, which was most of the time, or whenever an ambulance rattled past, impaling all the grace of the old city. He was a bit like an ox or bull or caged animal, he did everything with exaggerated drama, constantly raising his index and little fingers and pointing them towards the ground, another gesture intended to ward off evil. He drove a van and touched his balls when he drove past a cemetery or hospital or funeral hearse. His little Ape 50 (the name described not only the van but Salvatore himself) was in an advanced state of disintegration: it had no mirrors, and it couldn't go more than thirty-five kilometres an hour. Despite his life of abject misery, waking at five each day, facing the dark winter and the hellish summer, when merely to go outside was to sweat as though one had stepped into a sauna, in such conditions he would have to go down to farms and pick up produce, stack it, sell it, unwrap it, barter, sell, pack, unpack, all in the heat and the cold, with the mosquitoes and the barbarous sun and the humidity and the pollution and the noise and the scooters and the tourists that never left, never went home, and the imbecilic Florentines, who were so arrogant, so self-important, so rude (he himself was from Arezzo, which was an hour's drive from Florence), despite all this, and all the bills he had to pay and all the problems he had with his back and neck and his obsessive smoking that was killing his lungs, killing him, and the three litres of red wine he drank every day, which was killing his liver, he was a man who loved life. Although he loved life, he did not understand life, nor did he care to, nor did he think it was right to try to. Life was something that had been placed in front of us, like a steaming plate of ribbolita, and one either ate or turned the plate away. Only a foolish man would turn the plate away. He used to say, 'I eat when I am hungry and I eat when I am not, that is, I eat for the hunger that will come.'

Then he touched his balls.

Once when he had to drive his truck down one of the narrow stone roads in the city centre, he attached some large metal crates to the back of his truck. One of the crates had not been secured very well and shortly into the journey it started to shake and tremble and finally it freed itself and crashed onto the road towards the driver behind who managed to swerve and avoided hitting it. Salvatore, uncharacteristically, pulled over, realising he had done something wrong, and saw that the other driver had stopped too, and for once he was not angry, but was expecting someone else to take his anger out on him. Instead, the other driver was exceptionally civil and kind and seemed to accept what might have been a real disaster with philosophical resignation, so Salvatore embodied a kind of sentimental regret, a remorse, which was beautiful to behold, trying and failing to express his sadness, his gratitude, his appreciation for the driver's manners and good breeding. As they stood there discussing what had taken place with an attention to detail and a pedantry that was quite ridiculous, having parked their respective vehicles on the pavement, but still blocking the road because the road was so narrow, the accumulated cars started to let out a cacophony of demented, atonal sounds of horns and shouts of anger and curses in Italian, so that six or seven cars, gridlocked together, turned into one unit of anger. As Salvatore became aware of this, his own anger grew. He thought these drivers were impinging on this beautiful moment of understanding and tolerance and grace between himself and this mysterious, patient, saintly driver who seemed scarcely to be human – how could a man like that exist here in such a dog-eat-dog, such a ruthless, scurrying rat-shit world as this one – and for the drivers to do such a thing was unforgivable. Salvatore faced the cars and unleashed a torrent of abuse, a litany of swear words and curses and insults so elaborate as to be poetic, and in fact he tamed these drivers, raging against them, swelling like a gale force wind, generating more noise and rage than they were together able to do and so they were silenced and he won this impossible victory, his performance was so audacious, so pigheaded that in the end the drivers had to take their hats off in admiration, stilled by the sheer nerve of a man who was in the wrong but still managed to do battle with a line of cars.

He lived with a tiny woman, Gina, a scruffy, tough creature who had acquired a kind of hardness through the years that was like the hardness of leather after being exposed to rain and wind and dry heat and various blows and cuts and whips.

She had been squeezed through a sieve of bereavement and heartbreak so that what remained of her needed to be lubricated by kindness, like the etiolated limbs of a dying man for whom just to move requires a herculean effort. Salvatore was not the man to marinate her, he was scarcely able to marinate a pork chop in fact, but he found with her that at least she left him alone, to his own devices; she was not like other women he had known who had wanted to ensnare his very soul, to stick it in a jar, with pickled cucumbers and other dead things. She left him free to gamble on horses, to drink, to curse his mother, to make visits to whores.

One day Gina told him she was pregnant, which was a shock to say the least. Salvatore just sat there, staring like an idiot. He thought idly about how he should react, like someone looking through his wardrobe and thinking about which jacket to wear. None of his habitual, knee-jerk reactions seemed right this time, none of the jackets fitted. So he just sat there, staring like an idiot, which was what he was. He considered getting angry with her, asking her how she could have let something like this happen. How could something like this have happened at all. In the company of men, with men, life was easier, more straightforward, things fell into place; women came along and complicated everything with their make-up and high heels, their recipes and addictions to shopping, to fashions, to romantic ideas, with their periods, hidden vaginas, secretions, wombs that changed shape minute by minute, why did she have to get pregnant?

But when the baby (a boy) arrived, magically, magnificently, it had the effect of stilling Salvatore's disquiet. He stared at this thing, helpless and creased and wrinkled, how hideous and yet beautiful it looked, he thought, beauty that had its roots in the grotesque. He started looking at other babies, started noticing them, even commenting on them, making remarks to their proud mothers, then thinking of his own child when he was away from it, at the market, driving around, with his mates, missing it, feeling a rush of joy, as though someone had given him the most fantastic, complex toy in the world that would not get old but somehow day by day become more complex, more fantastic.

He took fatherhood seriously. He started to help Gina around the house, cleaned the sheets, ironed them. He stopped drinking as much, quit smoking altogether, and bought lots of things for his baby.

They decided to name the kid Oliver. When asked why he hadn't chosen Salvatore or an Italian name, at first he had no answer, but gradually one started to occur to him, deep down in his brain, though at first he did not perceive it as such, as an answer. He had the feeling that if he were to use an Anglo-Saxon name, his child would be better than he was, would be shorn of his loutishness and peasant lineage and brutishness. He wanted to produce a better, neater, cleverer version of himself.

So Oliver grew and gurgled, breast-fed and cried, though he cried quite rarely for a baby. Soon he became a smiling, angelic child, walking, waddling really, his hair as gentle and delicate as the feathers of an eider duck. Salvatore watched this thing in fascination, scarcely believing his eyes, and Oliver soon exceeded all his expectations. His brain was developing at an alarming rate and he was like some mad, growing vine in summer, growing stronger, more verdant and more elaborate at every angle and corner. By the time he was two he was reading, writing and speaking even words from other languages that he had picked up from television, sometimes even complete phrases, and when he spoke in these foreign tongues, wisps of English, French, German, his father grew disconcerted and thought his own child was making fun of him, but then he dismissed this thought. When he turned three, they both realised he had an extraordinary memory, for words, for language, for facts and figures, and he already knew by heart all sorts of statistics and geographical details. By the age of four he was playing a tiny violin that Gina had picked up at a flea market and they decided that he should take lessons and scraped together enough money to find a good, affordable teacher.

While all this was going on, Salvatore would introduce his friends, who were all simple, humble market folk, to his kid, but Oliver's obvious brilliance did not always go down so well, and Salvatore's friends were often stumped by the complicated questions the child would ask, sometimes of a philosophical nature. It seemed as though all of Plato and Shakespeare was contained – in simple form – within his brain. He would suck his thumb and say, in flawless Italian, 'Is this world a copy of another? Can we know God as we know a person? What is the ultimate purpose of life?' Soon these friends began to keep their distance from Salvatore and no longer felt comfortable around him and his wunderkind. In fact, they began to notice a difference in Salvatore himself, who no longer seemed interested in drinking wine or beer or smoking or playing the horses or recounting bawdy tales of visits to prostitutes and brothels and bars and race tracks, and even announced that he had started reading Dante, whom he had always loathed with a passion, and was attempting to write verse of his own, doggerel really, but light years away from anything he had hitherto attempted with his free time, light years away from riotous conversations at the trippa stand, and unruly nights at the football stadio, and afternoons in the Tuscan countryside tasting wine from barrels at inexpensive enotecas, and evenings spent in eating bistecca in Panzano. He began to read widely: St. Augustine, Boccaccio, Petrarch, and the events of his previous life seemed misty and insubstantial as though now he had truly caught sight of something real and lasting through the presence of his son, who provided evidence of some presiding deity and of the ineffable workings of the universe. He learnt to cook delicious meals, bought and arranged flowers, expressed an interest in travel and foreign cultures and started to take English lessons, so that he might converse with his kid who was by then already fluent in English and French and spoke some German and Spanish tolerably well.

Oliver had just turned four. His father sat down in the trattoria and and was greeted by the waiters in an almost deferential way. He waited for his antipasto. The tables were pushed close together which made it easy to get into conversations with the other diners. He took out a battered copy of the Canzoniere of Petrach and began to read, ignoring all the other customers and pouring, now and again, discreet amounts of red wine into a small glass. The trattoria was noisy and cramped and hot, but the food was excellent.

Not looking up from his book, he was aware of someone

next to him, then he was aware of the same person sitting down opposite him, a solitary diner like himself, who had to make do with sharing his table with a stranger. He didn't look up from his book until he had come to the end of the poem and he was taken aback to see someone he actually knew. Checking an impulse to greet him, he realised that the man across the table had no idea who Salvatore was. The newcomer looked straight ahead without the slightest flicker of recognition.

'Ubaldo, it's me, Salvatore, don't you know me?'

'Excuse me?'

'It's Salvatore, we used to have a glass of wine together at the Pizzicheria. At Antonio's place. Come on, you must remember?'

'Oh! Salvatore, Good God, I wouldn't have known you . . . you look . . . you've changed completely, how long's it been? But . . . well, come to think of it, you look exactly the same.'

'So, how is it you didn't recognise me?'

'I don't know, it's a weird thing, you are the same, and yet not the same. I can't say what it is exactly, you just . . .'

'Yes?'

'Have you been getting laid?'

Salvatore laughed exuberantly and gave Ubaldo a hearty pat on the back.

'You still working on your PhD? Philosophy? Undiscovered genius? How's that going?'

'Shit. I keep running out of money. What's the point of a PhD in philosophy, how the hell am I going to find a job afterwards? Much better to get laid, like you.'

Salvatore explained that he hadn't been having sex, that he was no longer much interested in sex, then the newcomer

## The Balls

said he envied him and that sex was all he ever thought about. Salvatore suggested that Ubaldo try and seduce one of the young American students who roamed the streets of Florence. Ubaldo said that he didn't feel like it and that he would probably soon have to pay a visit to the Cascine park, where the ladies of the night were to be found. Salvatore said, 'It's such an uneven, unbalanced arrangement: the client hardly ever fucks and the whore does nothing but fuck.' Their food arrived and they tucked in, happy not to be dining alone.

In between mouthfuls, Ubaldo said, 'So tell me, what have you been up to?'

'Oh, you know, the usual, this and that.'

'You still at the market?'

'Sure.'

'All ok there?'

'Yeah, all ok. Been growing my own stuff, got some wonderful cauliflowers.'

'Really?'

'They're beautiful, don't you think?'

'I suppose so, never really thought about it.'

'They remind me of the brain, their shape.'

'I suppose so,' said Ubaldo. He scooped up the last strands of his spaghetti greedily.

'You still with Gina?' he asked, slightly hesitantly.

'Yeah, we're still together, she's not such a bad girl. Rotten teeth but good heart.'

'You still play the horses?'

'No, not really, I got a bit fed up with all that. Trying to improve myself now, trying to think about other things, focus on other horizons, other vistas. I'm a bit more . . . bit more even . . . more solid . . . these days.'

'It's true . . . I hardly recognised you, you seem so . . . another man, a newer one, or something. Saul on the way to Damascus, maybe?'

'Maybe. Well Ubaldo, maybe you hit the nail on the head. Let's have a drink, let's toast to good food, good women, to goodness.'

They clinked glasses, Ubaldo staring at Salvatore as if for the first time. He shakily drained the contents of his glass and poured himself more wine and drained that as well.

'So you got tired of the horses?' he asked, feeling slightly better.

'I did. Tired? No, not tired, not exactly, I just no longer saw the need for gambling, for the rush of excitement, maybe I outgrew it. Maybe I saw the horses in a different light, maybe I saw that it was cruel to whip them, just to get them to run faster. Maybe I was looking for excitement, something to take my mind off my problems, well, it worked for a while . . . but then . . . something changed.'

'What happened?'

'Nothing . . . I mean, nothing that I could put into words. Life happened. And everything grew very simple and very beautiful and very calm. And everything made sense. For the first time. And I perceived the beauty, the joy, the sanity of the world that was previously hidden to me. And I looked at old, hidden streets where I'd wandered for hours, looking for fights, looking for love, finding nothing, just a big hole, then I walked back to streets I'd never noticed, that had never interested me, and this time I found something there. I'd always been searching in the wrong place, mistaking shadows for real forms. Let's have another drink.'

Ubaldo nodded and said, 'You know, it's almost as if you

are uttering my own thoughts. It all sounds so familiar to me,' said Ubaldo, deeply and genuinely impressed. He poured Salvatore a glass of wine and waited, waited.

'You know, seeing you like this, so . . . different. Well, I'd like to tell you something.'

'Go ahead,' Salvatore mumbled, his mouth full of polenta.

'I really can't get over how you've changed. I mean, you've really . . . you're floating . . . like . . . a balloon . . . you're suddenly airborne . . . you're floating above the earth.'

'Can you pass me the salt?'

'Willingly. It's like I look at you and I see . . . it's like you've become enlightened and you are up there in the sky, while we poor fuckers are still floundering about down here in the sewer.'

'Don't exaggerate, come on. You're not in the sewer. You're smart as hell, you have a brilliant mind. You know that, don't you?'

'Maybe. Maybe I did have once. Before I ruined it . . . I don't know, I feel like I could tell you anything and you would understand, that you would accept it all with grace and compassion, like a real philosopher, like a yogi.'

'Compassion is the hardest thing, only the Buddha had compassion, compassion towards all living things. The Buddha, maybe a few others. That's about it.'

'You know, Salvatore, I've been carrying a secret around with me for years. And I've never been able to . . . to tell . . . anyone.'

'Go ahead. It's true you can tell me anything. You are right about that.'

'Actually, I should re-phrase that. I've never been able to tell *you*.'

'Me?'

'Well, actually yes, it concerns you. Maybe now I can finally get it off my chest. I think I would feel a lot lighter, better inside.'

'Well, you've certainly got my attention now.'

Salvatore smiled and it was at once gentle, luminous, forgiving. Ubaldo stared at him in silence, confident enough to go ahead and just say it, without apology or lies, his pathway lit and guided by Salvatore's benign smile, convinced of a positive outcome.

'I think I should just come right out with it . . . . Ok, so here goes. I once fucked Gina.'

'Oh.'

Salvatore glanced at the remains of his polenta. It looked rather sickening.

'When was this?' Salvatore asked evenly.

'Well, it would have been close to five years ago, I guess.'

Salvatore stared at Ubaldo. He didn't say anything. For a moment he looked utterly depleted of strength. Then his brow furrowed and he seemed to be wrestling with some titanic, unseen enemy. He was gradually smitten with the realisation that it was the man in front of him whose sperm had fertilised Gina's egg and so created the child who had utterly transformed his life and himself, in fact his actual identity, over the past four years. So, in some awful way, he owed his own rebirth to this man's successful insemination of Gina, to this man's genes. It was intolerable to realise that not only was he not Oliver's biological father, but that Oliver's brilliance was in no way attributable to himself. And even that wasn't the end of it: he had recreated himself because of an illusion, a complete and utter falsehood. He owed his new self then to this man seated opposite him; this man opposite him who was, in a terrible and shocking way, the progenitor of his *vita nuova*, his new life. He felt a violent rush shoot up from his bowels to his brain, rising like mercury at the touch of heat. He knew that he had to destroy this man, or at least harm him beyond repair, only then could he be in peace. At once his old self came crashing back, obliterating all traces of reasoning and civility and cultivation, and it felt good, it felt really, really fucking great to lunge at Ubaldo, to lash out and tear at him as if he was some great bear about to rip its victim apart. As his great body rose and grabbed at Ubaldo, the other diners, shaking themselves out of their stupor, lunged at Salvatore and tried to hold him back from his pale, sick, shaken victim, but he had the strength of ten men and it was all they could do to form a wall between him and Ubaldo, panting and cowering and crying. Salvatore was like some great river that had burst its banks: he seemed to be everywhere, all over the restaurant, as he heaved and growled. They managed to pull him down and wrestled him to the floor and he lay there, supine and frantic, and someone, a burly man in a brown leather jacket, pinned his feet to the ground until they eventually ceased their frantic motion. It was as though the burly man was suffocating his feet and then they succumbed to stillness. Salvatore signalled that he would be quiet now, and he asked if someone could fetch him a drop of water. But the men still surrounded him. Nobody moved. The place was dangerously silent. A minute passed. Finally, apparently convinced of Salvatore's exhaustion and compliance, the men made the fatal mistake of relaxing their grip. With an almighty effort Salvatore rose, ripped through the human fence, grabbed a fork from a table and stabbed Ubaldo directly in the testicles. The fork impaled him, pinned into his linen pants like some metallic erection. Ubaldo screamed like a stuck pig and the whole party of diners was convulsed in horror. Agony. Flames. Hell. The backdrop of blood and madness in the midst of dishes of spaghetti and polenta. It was pitiful. It was dreadful. Despair rose from the black, sooty bowels of life and threatened to throttle it like some great boa constrictor.

Shortly afterwards the police arrived and Salvatore was carted away. Ubaldo recovered in hospital, but he was never able to have sex again. He abandoned his PhD and became a cashier at a supermarket. Gina brought fruit, chiefly oranges, to Salvatore in jail and eventually Oliver met his real, vandalized father, whom he instantly liked.

So there was a kind of happy ending to the whole sorry bloody mess, I suppose.

# THE VISITATION

THE THING APPEARED very early in the morning, just as summer was starting to arrive. It appeared on a Cornish beach like an ejected monstrosity. As the waves roared and frothed and a few bits of debris were brought up to the shore like torn fragments of memory, a terrifying apparition was unveiled. It resembled a kind of roasted pig, but instead of having hooves it had toes. Its ghastly jaw was pinned back in bloated, sardonic glee. Its paws were strung out and seemed to want to inch towards the wary and nauseated onlooker. What was it? Maybe it was a dog, or a raccoon, or gigantic rat. Or maybe it was some kind of bizarre mutation, the result of some sick experiment conducted by mad scientists trying to join different animals together. Had the thing been assembled from different body parts, fused together? And had the sea's salt water eventually caused all cracks and joins to fade away, to vanish?

The fishermen who were out at that early hour had seen plenty of horrible things in their time, but this they hadn't experienced. They stood and watched it and tried to shake off their unease.

Rufus, an existential younger fisherman, who had only recently joined the ranks of the others, reached for his flask and took a quick sip of whisky. To think that these monsters exist down there in the depths, and we skirt the surface each day not knowing what the hell we are skirting on top of, not knowing what we are inches or miles away from.

'The thing's a raccoon, I tell you,' sunburnt Jago insisted.

'There are no raccoons in Cornwall, or in the British Isles, for that matter,' Smudge declared authoritatively.

'Must have been washed in from the New World,' said Rob Ager.

'You aren't trying to tell me that thing has come all the way from America?' said Jago.

'That's precisely what I'm trying to tell you,' said Rob Ager.

'It's not possible. There's no way its body would be intact after such a long voyage. It's conceivable that it might have come over from Germany – they have raccoons in Germany,' said Smudge.

'It's not a raccoon,' said Rufus.

'So what is it?'

'I'm buggered if I know.'

'It's a hybrid, like a minotaur: half pig, half dog. The thing to put fear in the hearts of men. It has arrived. The thing to switch off our brains,' Mewts proclaimed, the autodidact and scholar of the group.

Rufus went up to the thing and prodded at it with a stick. Thank God it was dead, though he had his doubts.

'Was the darn thing glued together? Like Frankenstein's monster? Or one of Simo Simos's kebabs?'

Nobody said anything. These were fishermen, they were not equipped to deal with the idea of man-made mutations coming into existence. Grotesque distortions. Freakish nightmares. Rufus took out his tobacco and began to roll himself a cigarette.

'Let's get ourselves some breakfast, I want to get away from here for a while.'

*The Visitation*

'The boy's right. We'll go down to The Greasy Fork. There's no catch to be had right now.'

The party of unlikely looking companions, all grizzled and bedraggled with straggly beards and tattooed arms and shuffling gaits, began to make their way to the café in search of wholesome eggs and bacon to banish the spectre of the monster. The early morning breeze was invigorating and the Cornish coast was lighting up to magnificent effect.

'There's no point in torturing yourself about some nameless creature,' Mewts the scholar said to Rufus, as though reading his mind. 'There are more things in heaven and earth than are dreamt of in our bloody philosophies, boy. Some things we will never know nor understand. That's the life we have. Swim with it, don't fight against the current. You will never get any answers, mark my words. Let's have some breakfast and a mug or seven of industrial tea.'

'I suppose you're right. No answers, just questions. That thing has spooked me though. But the sea must be filled to bursting with such pig fish, goat fish, monkey fish. Can you imagine?'

'I prefer to think of its wonder and its beauty, lad. My boy, you have to understand that if you keep on looking at shadows, you won't see the sun.'

They arrived at The Greasy Fork and poured in unceremoniously. Molly, a large lady of indeterminate age, was delighted to see them and set to work immediately on the preparation of six breakfasts. They smoked, they chattered, the place became a centre of gossip, a vehicle for vulgarity.

'Simon Trollin told me a queer thing. His nephew's girlfriend may be pregnant. She's only twelve, just goes to show.'

'In the opinion of many, Fred Creasey is addicted to crack.'

'Jenifer Peat has taken a lover: she's a woman.'

'If I were a woman, I would make love to women.'

'If you were a woman, I would stop liking women.'

What else floated down there in that darkness, Rufus thought, unable to take part in the banter. How many other disturbing things went on in this world that never came to be known about or talked about. Yes, we heard about the natural disasters, the hurricanes and the tsunamis, which crushed houses and cars and buildings like matchsticks. But they were all visible, the obvious signs of a world that was out of joint, lilting, sinking, capsizing. But maybe the other terrors, the invisible ones, those that took place off stage, in the wings, maybe they were altogether more sinister because not only would we fail to understand them, we wouldn't even know they had occurred. Now the world was moving too quickly and the unholy brew was running into little innumerable rivulets, seeping into every crack, turning everything into one gigantic landscape of the cobbled together, the genetically modified, the impure and the man-made. How long did we have left, how long before we would finally pollute every sea and lake and kill every animal and chop down every tree?

The scholar looked at him, wolfing down a choicely skewered piece of bacon on bread and egg, and grumbled between mouthfuls, 'You're at it again, Rufus boy, I've told you before now. Switch off the old grey cells or have a nip of whisky. It's no good you worrying all hours of the day. The world will take care of itself. It's us we should be worried about. Old mother earth, she's a tough old boot. Nothing we can do to touch her.'

'We're being phased out, aren't we?'

'That we are, my young sailor. Getting ready to be put

back in the cupboard. I don't much fancy our chances. Not enough lifeboats, not enough gear, just room for a life vest or two and then, bon voyage, my dears!'

The others continued to joke and stuff their faces and pour and drink tea and roll cigarettes and arm wrestle half jokingly and watch the line of the sea in the distance, somnolent and magnificent, testament to something that was, finally, beyond compromise, beyond the transitory borders of change and meaningless fashion. People could still see the sea, but how long before it too would eventually be obscured from view?

※

His girlfriend was renting a small room in the Trevose Head lighthouse cottages. The lighthouse, west of Padstow, sat perched, solitary on the edge of the land, rising above clusters of gnarled rocks and a perpetually snarling, crashing sea that pulled the onlooker into its vertiginous vortex.

She was wild, untethered and her life only made sense when she was entwined in his limbs or was running her hand through his dark, thick hair. He carried her into her room; the windows were flung open, but the room was filled with the smell of incense. They were smiling mischievously. They barely spoke as she undressed him, the land, the smell of the sea all over him, which she loved, it was as though she were making love to the sea. A strong wind rushed through the room as their lovemaking intensified and time slowed.

In her little den there wasn't an inch of free wall space; she had covered it with photographs and postcards and the effect was rich and intense. From a hook in the ceiling a brightly painted marionette bounced. Oranges were everywhere, squeezed into corners, and afterwards he reached for one and began peeling it, slowly lowering a segment into her expectant mouth. This was what it was always like between them, they didn't speak much, they were happy just to peer into each other's eyes and smile.

The strong beam of the lighthouse pulsed outwards and began its slow circumnavigation of the sea in a final, neutralising attempt to keep the forces of destruction at bay. He watched as patches of the dark sea were systematically illuminated, then cast into shadow.

'My love,' she whispered, 'did you think . . . you would find me . . . ever. One like me?'

He smiled and gently pulled each of her fingers in turn in a habitual gesture. 'I didn't think . . . I would find anyone . . . at all . . .'

'But you have such a heart, and are so sweet and good . . . how could you have thought such a thing?'

'I didn't see the sun. Mewts is always saying I spend too much time looking at shadows. I should be more like you, my little fairy.'

'Oh Rufus, I don't understand you, I really don't. Life is so beautiful, can you not see it? Taste it? Look outside . . . at that. Tell me what you see.'

He seemed to be deep in thought. The night's audio-visual intensity was all engulfing. He scrunched his eyes up and took some deep breaths.

'I'm a fisherman, I can't afford to be too romantic, Julie. You can live here by the sea and smell the salt breeze. But I have to be tough. I live on the sea. It's rough out there when the old girl is angry or has no gifts to give apart from a bit of blood. Feel these hands of mine.'

'I love your hands, Rufus, they undress my heart. My strength comes from these hands.'

'The net, the rope, that's what marinates these hands, gives them little gifts of calluses and creases.'

They kissed again. They watched the light, the long light of the beam as it continued its tireless rotation like the gigantically elongated blade of a helicopter gaining weird intensity.

Then : – a glitch, which, though it occupied in time barely a second, by its very nature seemed at once to subsequently balloon and straddle great gulfs and chasms of empty time, time that had consequently been suspended, had ground to a halt, and the light of the beam was extinguished and they could hear the motor that was moving it stop with a dead sound that chilled them to the bone.

'Rufus, what happened?'

'I can't think. Christ, that's weird. I should call the coast guard. Must be some kind of power failure or something. But that's strange because it hasn't touched the room's lights. Unless . . . I don't get it.'

He reached for the landline, but it was dead, and at once he was revisited by the dread of the morning. He stabbed repeatedly at the receiver but there was no dialling tone. 'Julie, it's strange but there's no line. Maybe we should go down to Padstow. Come on, we'll hop on my motorbike.'

'Rufus, are you sure? I'm awfully tired.'

'I should go at least and tell them. If the lighthouse is playing up someone should know.'

'All right, yes I suppose you are right. I'll come too. I don't want you to go alone, not when it's so late.'

They were getting ready to dress when another strange thing happened. The whole visible area of sea, that had been plunged into darkness upon the extinguishing of the lightbeam, began to shimmer with a brilliant, intoxicating light that had no visible source. Soon the surface of a great stretch of water was as radiant as if the morning sun was flinging its beams upon it. They stared at this mad enchantment in absolute terror: nature seemed to have gone into an inverted meltdown, the logic of night and day, of linear time had been upended. Rufus felt his skin freeze over as he tightly held his beloved Julie, wondering what was happening, trying frantically to understand, searching for the moon, for some signal in the night sky that would offer an explanation, a plane, a shooting star, anything, but there was nothing, no signal or sign. They tightly held onto one another, wondering whether they were witnessing the end of the world. Then the light was pulled back, as if by a gigantic hand, and the sea's surface cast back once more into darkness. They found that they were both breathing very quickly and that their hearts were racing at insane rates. The beauty of the spectacle registered, for what they had both witnessed made the world's greatest firework display somehow pale into insignificance. With a jolt, a dull mechanical registration, the lighthouse beam switched itself on and began to revolve as it had always done.

Julie lit a cigarette and Rufus joined her and for a while they just smoked in silence, still scared, and yet grateful for what they could conceive of only in terms of something miraculous. They stubbed out their cigarettes, knocked sideways by exhaustion and went to sleep, feeling strangely safe and warm and cosy.

Two weeks later Mewts was reading through an article in the *St Ives Times and Echo* whilst devouring a hearty breakfast in The Greasy Fork.

## Case of Mystery Animals Continues

The Cornish community remains baffled by the case of the mystery animals being washed up on the beaches of Penzane. The animals, which have not as yet been properly identified, seem to resemble pigs but have toes instead of hooves. Onlookers who have spotted these dead creatures have variously claimed them to be dogs, or even giant rats.

The case continues to command great interest and Penzane has been flooded with tourists hoping to catch a glimpse of one of these 'monsters'. The local fishing community professes to be absolutely baffled and cannot understand what these creatures actually are. It has been suggested that their obvious exposure to water over long periods of time has caused bloating and made the creatures unrecognisable, and the fact that they are in a state of advanced decomposition might account for their grotesque appearance, but this theory does not explain the anatomical abnormalities in their carcasses.

Douglas Wilson, a researcher from Glasgow University studying abnormalities in animal genes and genetic makeup, has examined several of these animals and drawn some disturbing conclusions.

'I have studied these creatures now over several weeks and performed autopsies on their internal organs, and whilst they do bear certain resemblances to creatures we know and love, like dogs and pigs, I can tell you that there are far too many anatomical discrepancies for us to be able to actually identify them properly. It seems inevitable to me – however far-fetched it may sound – to conclude that these animals are not of terrestrial origin.'

When this newspaper pressed Grant E. Gordon, an environmental spokesman for the government, for a statement on this matter, he declined to comment.

# ALBA

I

A LBA HAD TWO lovers. One was public, the other secret. Neither of them knew of the other's existence.

Alba was twenty-nine, and lived with her mother in a small ossified village in Calabria. Her beauty was unkempt, almost savage. Men smiled at her and when she smiled back, they instantly fell in love with her. They watched her as she walked away and tried to postpone the moment of her vanishing.

Her old mother was a seamstress; her father was dead from alcohol. Alba worked as a waitress, but didn't make enough to pay her bills. She was learning to listen to the music of the universe when her solitude and poverty weighed heavily on her. She dreamed of saving enough – not much, just four thousand euros – to go to New York and work there as a dish washer, as anything, but she knew no English and she couldn't see a way of severing her ties with her mother.

Alba's secret lover was Pasquale. Whenever Alba and Pasquale made love, he touched her reverentially, as though she was a precious parchment about to crumble into dust. Alba's feelings about his reverence were complex: she loved it, and it made her uneasy.

One night as they lay together in his bedroom, Pasquale's hands entwined in hers, she said, 'Sometimes I think you are in love with a sense of me as someone else, sometimes I think you don't know me at all.'

'What do you mean?'

'Well, maybe you think too highly of me. Maybe you think I'm much better than I am.'

'I see you at your best. When we are together, I see all your wonderful qualities shining. I dreamt about you two days ago. I didn't tell you.'

'Why not?'

Pasquale was silent. Outside they could hear the sound of a barrel organ playing tuneless winding music. The man turning the wheel was doing so with his one remaining arm. Sunburnt Calabrians sat in the village square, outside the bar, sipping their espressos, smoking cigarettes, puzzling about how the glorious valley of youth had become the cracked basin of age.

'What happened in your dream?'

'We were together, you were glowing with the sun, and had flowers in your hair. We were at peace with one another; we were happy together.'

Alba leant over and kissed him very gently. Pasquale wrapped his arms around her, feeling a newly created place inside himself, a place that he feared would eventually be closed off and sealed. He whispered, 'In my arms, you are even more lovely.' She smiled with irrepressible joy; her olive skin and dark eyes, her pitch-black hair radiated heat. His words reached deep into her soul and offered it a priceless balm.

She faced him. 'Your voice sings to me, my prince.'

Soon though she yearned for the more rugged body of Mario and his disrespectful coal-black eyes. Mario's treatment of her was far from romantic; at times he was even rough with her. They would make love in all positions. With him sex was vulgar, corrosive, blasphemous. He brought her no flowers, never paid her compliments, never caressed her. He was her official boyfriend but they rarely spoke, often sitting in silence. Yet something tied them together, strong and unquestioned, like the wind or fire.

Mario opened a bottle of wine, poured a glass and offered it to Alba. Though not an obviously tender or meaningful gesture, she found it touching. She placed it to her lips, looked into his dark eyes, wishing, yearning he would say something sweet and poetic to her. Or say anything at all. Instead he poured himself a glass and produced a tissue and wiped the rim of the bottle very gently, choosing to lavish his care on an inanimate object.

'There's something wrong with my car,' he said. 'I took it to the mechanic. A dispersion of the current.'

'Oh, what's that?'

'It means the battery's power is being sucked away by something. They are damned if they know what it is. Maybe I should get rid of it. Maybe it's had its day.'

'No, please don't do that. I love that car.'

'If you say so. But a car's a car, not a person. You get too attached to things, Alba.'

She scrambled around for a cigarette. His big hands moved and fluttered along the table, like birds too damaged to fly.

Alba regarded him implacably and drank her wine.

'Why do you never speak?'

'What are you talking about? I just spoke about my car.'

'Why do you never speak about things that matter?'

'Such as?'

'How you feel, your feelings for me, for life. Nature. Beauty.'

'I don't understand.'

'No, I didn't think you would.'

Alba was getting more and more frustrated with Mario, but somehow she needed him. He was the rock her waves could crash against. She had to be very careful to juggle her two lovers, especially in the village, where everyone knew everyone's minutest habits and gossiped. Mario looked at Alba searchingly as though trying to read her mind. He felt tenderness rising up and enveloping him with its paradoxical force. He was on the verge on saying something. But then he thought better of it and poured himself more wine.

In the local bar Alba sat sipping coffee, flicking through a magazine, rehearsing in her mind some different dance steps a Greek had once shown her. One of the locals, an Albanian with an enormous stomach, entered the shop and as usual complimented Alba on her beauty. He launched into a monologue: 'I'm up at 6 every day, this heat, Dio buono, life without women is no life at all, give me a grappa, Marta my dearest, Madonna this heat.' From behind the counter the grilled face of Marta stared back at him with her customary cynicism.

Alba ran through the dance numbers in her mind again. Her cell phone started vibrating. A text message said, 'The thought of you makes this life more pleasant, more light, more wonderful, Pasquale.' She smiled, wondering how it was that her two men could be so very different. She asked herself which one she ultimately preferred. Pasquale was so sensitive as to almost be like a faithful dog. Mario was so inscrutable as to almost be like a tree. Pasquale is more important to me so I should be with him, but Mario is my rock that my waves can crash against. If I crashed against Pasquale, he would be swept away.

*Alba*

The Albanian launched into an old refrain. 'Women don't like too much talk, they like a bit of slap and tickle. There's never been a woman born that I can't satisfy, I give them a good seeing to, they go home happy.' Marta said, 'Oy oy,' very audibly and lit a cigarette with exhausted relish. Some stray dogs, lost or abandoned, entered the bar, apparently to see if anything was afoot. Alba instantly went to caress them with extraordinary tenderness. The Albanian watched in awe. Alba remembered she had promised to make meatballs for Mario. It was a matter of great importance to her that the meatballs were excellent. She paid for her coffee and rehearsed a little dance move; Marta applauded in delight.

Alba walked unhurriedly through the golden streets, charmed by the little flowers pinned to the street lamps, moved by the sight of the setting sun, thinking of the sweetness of Pasquale's text message and wondering whether she would ever get Mario to reveal something about his inner life. She felt convinced that he had things to say, it simply wasn't possible that he was completely empty inside. Maybe he had built a wall of concrete around himself in order to get through life, to get through an exhausting job as a blacksmith that required him to wake up at five every morning. But maybe now that concrete could never be stripped away. All at once the meatballs no longer seemed that important. She dialled his number. When he answered, she spoke hesitantly, 'Could we go out for dinner tonight instead of having meatballs?'

'Why?'

'I just don't feel like staying in. We could go to the trattoria. I don't feel like cooking.'

'Whatever you say.'

'Is that ok?'

'Alba . . . I was thinking . . . about how you say that I never speak. Perhaps it's true. I want to speak more with you. I want to speak about those things that you talked about . . . .'

'That's . . . that's wonderful Mario! Oh, I'm so pleased.'

The impulse to make meatballs again for him re-asserted itself.

'Let's stay in after all. I'll make you meatballs and we can talk, we can talk the whole night long. I'll light candles and we can have a nice romantic dinner. How does that sound?'

'The football's on later. We could watch the game.'

Alba listened, hanging her head.

'Yes, all right.'

'Alba?'

'Yes?'

'You're a strange girl.'

'I know, Mario.'

She slid the cell phone into her pocket. She felt a pang of guilt for deceiving him, for sleeping with another man. And yet it seemed she had no choice in the matter. A shrivelled old lady in shawls was hobbling painfully up towards the church. Alba watched her until she was safely inside. Then she began walking home.

Later that week, Pasquale and Alba stood next to each other in his bedroom. Alba said, 'I'm smaller than you are. But when I think of us together, somehow I think I'm taller than I really am.'

Pasquale said, 'Can I explain something to you?'

She nodded, patiently.

'I know about the other man you are seeing.'

She started to blush, and became flustered.

'But how?'

'The other day I was standing outside your apartment block, I was thinking of surprising you. I had some flowers for you. I knew that your mother was at work.

'I was just about to ring the bell when I saw him. He was there, standing next to me. I moved away. I could sense something. It's difficult to explain, but I knew he was there to see you. He turned to look at me. I muttered something about how I'd made a mistake and that this wasn't the address I was looking for. I looked into his eyes – I could see you in them. Then I walked away. I always feared you had another man.'

'It's true, I don't know what to say. I'm ashamed.'

'Don't be. I love you. And for me love means acceptance. I love you so much. I won't let anyone or anything hurt you.'

Alba looked at him, as if seeing him for the first time.

'Who should I thank for meeting you? You are the best man I have ever known.'

'Be with me, stay with me. Let's get married.'

Her eyes instantly filled with tears. The tears changed the texture of everything, even of the air between them.

'I can't. It wouldn't work. Soon you would start to despise me. I can't – not now. I have to be free for a while. At least.'

He nodded, but he didn't understand.

'You see, it's just that . . . sometimes this darkness comes over me . . . and then my heart is heavy, yet empty. I love life, I do . . . the trees, the ocean, the animals, the fishes in the sea. They are all so beautiful, so very beautiful. But this darkness sometimes . . . chokes me . . . .'

'What is it, Alba? What is it?'

She made no reply.

## 2

Alba drove her little Fiat down a country road, all windows open, the lyrical voice of Fabrizio de André filling the hot car. The air conditioning was broken and she didn't have money to have it fixed. The sun, a great gaseous orb, hurled itself against the earth. She dreamed of leaving her dead village. The people were always the same, watching her every move; the food, the weather was always the same. The post office was a gossip office. Standing in line for hours to get the simplest things done: to pay a bill, to send a letter. Hearing how Ferruzzano, the notary, had cheated someone or how Morabito, the plumber, had money stashed away. Alba dreamed again of New York and all its promise of anonymous freedom.

She stopped the car in front of a tree. She was in an abandoned field, off the main road. There must be more to life than this, she thought. Why did I have to be born here, where no one ever comes and no one ever goes? If only I'd been born in Milan. Or Rome. I have no father and my mother is old. Soon I'll be old and I'll still be here, in this village, watching the men playing cards.

A stray dog walked up to her. Poor thing, it looked sick and gaunt. She didn't even have a bottle of water for it. Maybe it was too late for her, for the dog. She pulled out her mobile phone, thinking of Pasquale, about his offer of marriage. Would he go with her to America?

The small dog started whimpering; the thought crossed her mind that he was putting on an act for her. But from its desiccated mouth and eyes she knew it wasn't. She started stroking it, and saying kind words, trying her best to comfort it. Almost immediately the dog grew less agitated. She pulled it up to her, cradling it, scanning the surrounding countryside for some sign of life. She found nothing. They got in the car and she started the engine. The dog was ailing in the inescapable heat. She drove fast to generate some wind, her companion breathing rapidly and erratically. Eventually they came in sight of a bar and she prayed it was open. It was. She carried the dog inside. There she was received by no one. The blinding sunlight gave way to a black void and she had to grope about as her eyes slowly adjusted to it. The place smelled stuffy with neglect and decay.

Two or three empty espresso cups stood on the bar, a couple of sandwiches putrefied under glass. 'Anyone here?' she called out. There were no sounds of approaching footsteps. Everything was unnaturally still. She walked around to the back of the counter, ran a tap and filled a glass of water for the dog and placed it to its mouth and it glugged the whole lot down, instantly reviving.

'*Come sei bello, sei buono, bravo. Stai meglio ora, no?*' She sat down on a stool and waited till he had finished, then she refilled the glass. Her eye caught sight of a small metallic box sitting under a thick file, squeezed into an alcove beneath the cash till. It was a security box. She stared at it. For an awful moment she was tempted. Maybe this box was meant for her? She pulled it out, looking around furtively. No one came. To her amazement the box was unlocked. It opened easily. Inside there sat a fat wad of fifty-euro notes. She saw it all now. The drive, the dog who had brought her here, the box full of money. The money, it was meant for her. She was sure of it. Without hesitation she stuffed all the notes inside her pocket. At that moment an extraordinary unreality permeated everything. She might have been in a mine, miles below the earth. Or in a catacomb. She caught a glimpse of herself in a mirror: she appeared as a pallid, waxwork doll shrinking and shrivelling up like the burning stump of a candle. She moved towards the door. The dog, realising his new, beautiful mistress was about to abandon him, whimpered. In a trance of numbness, she strode over to him, plucked him up and they left.

Inside the car the numbness abated. She pulled out the cash and started counting. Nine hundred and fifty euros. She started the engine. This was the best thing that had happened to her in years and she was determined to celebrate. But who with? Pasquale? Or Mario? Both? Mario would kill Pasquale if he knew about him. And Pasquale? He would be okay with Mario, friendly even. The dog started licking her face. She wished that the money was dog food, but it wasn't. She stepped hard on the accelerator, singing ecstatically to Fabrizio de André. She drove the car hard, its engine was strained to the limit. She drove, planning on what she would do with the money, amazed by her lack of guilt, and her euphoria transmitted to her dog and together they were good companions and he barked in happiness, so pleased to have a new, beautiful owner. But she faltered and lost control of the steering wheel; the car spun off the road and went crashing into a massive tree, its bonnet instantly crushed. Alba was hurtled against the wheel and her face impacted with terrible force into it. Black smoke spilled out of the ruined car and Alba lay there unconscious. Her dog barked until it couldn't bark anymore.

While Alba was lying there, her face bloodied and smashed, her car written off, the glorious Calabrian countryside was still and silent, baking in the middle of the afternoon. No bird sang for Alba, no cloud ceased to move, no tree shed leaves for her. It mattered little to Nature whether Alba lived or died. Alba had worries and cares and loves and joys, but the universe was not interested in them. She just lay there, suspended between life and death.

No other car passed for a time, then a black Fiat Punto appeared. The driver slowed down, took a good, hard look at the scene of the crash and decided to continue on his way. He didn't want any complications, and besides, the woman was probably dead, he reasoned.

Fifteen minutes later, a red Lancia rounded the corner and the horrified driver stopped, got out and dialled for an ambulance with his mobile phone. By then the dog had stopped barking and had fallen into a sickly sleep. The driver yanked the car door open and felt for Alba's pulse. He couldn't find it. He had a mirror in the glove compartment of his car. He fetched it and placed it next to her mouth. She was still breathing. He wondered whether he should move Alba from her position; he wasn't sure whether to do so would endanger her life further, deciding in the end it was best not to touch her. The man stared at her bloodied face in sadness. The remnants of her beauty could still be discerned, as though a faint light was attempting to break through gauze. Eventually the light dimmed until it was only a barely perceptible quiescence, like her fading heartbeat.

The ambulance came. The paramedics carefully extracted her limp body and sped off. The dog went with them. The man remained. Eventually he walked slowly back to his car. Life's fragility, previously shrouded, had revealed itself: an outline as unmistakable as the distant olive trees during his slow, careful drive home.

3

In the intensive care unit of the Santa Maria Spina Hospital, Alba was linked up to many tubes and drips. The *carabinieri* were there. They had identified the patient from her driving license and they were carefully perusing the numbers stored on her phone. The senior officer had found the money in Alba's trouser pocket, his suspicions instantly alerted by the sum. He decided that investigating the matter further could wait.

As he was considering calling Alba's mother, whose number was listed under MAMMA, her phone started vibrating. He could see that someone called CHIARA was ringing, so he answered: 'Pronto', and was surprised to hear a man's voice on the other end. It was Pasquale. Alba had stored his number under a woman's name so as to divert suspicion from Mario if he were to check her calls. Pasquale was also surprised to find Alba's phone being answered by a man and he wondered if it was Mario, who had discovered the truth about them, and at once he became anguished at the thought of losing her.

The senior officer, for his part, being Calabrian and shrewd, immediately put two and two together and realised that whoever it was on the other end of the line was a secret in the patient's life. But that was not his business and, in any case, the man had a right to know what had happened to her. So he told him. The anguish that Pasquale had felt at the possibility of losing Alba was nothing compared to the darkness that now enveloped him. His voice and life entered a dismal tunnel from which they would not emerge for weeks. Pasquale asked for the hospital's name and, in a decrepit whisper, said he would be there as soon as he could. The officer then realised that the number stored under AMORE was obviously that of Alba's official *fidanzato* and he experienced a moment of hesitation. He wondered whether he should call the boyfriend and thereby bring the latter face to face with his probable rival. Nevertheless, he called Mario, who listened to the terrible news with extraordinary reserves of strength and told the officer he was leaving immediately. Finally the grim task of calling Alba's mother remained and the police officer, knowing the special bond between an Italian mother and her daughter, took a moment to collect himself and then called, speaking as gently and clearly as possible.

'Signora, I have some bad news. There's been an accident. Unfortunately your daughter has been badly injured, but her condition is stable.'

At first Alba's mother simply could not comprehend what was being said to her. Then the officer explained again. She could not form words but she understood. She had been peeling potatoes in the kitchen and she grabbed a small wooden table to stop herself from collapsing. She managed to flop onto her chair and began sobbing quietly. She could not bring herself to connect what the man on the telephone was saying with Alba, with her Alba, the most beautiful girl in the village. The police officer asked for her address and said a car would be along to fetch her. Alba's mother sat, staring at the unfinished potatoes, wishing she herself had been in the accident and not her beautiful daughter, who was still beginning her life. Memories from Alba's golden youth paraded before her old, cataracted eyes, a dazzling tapestry of promise, now viciously lacerated.

When the police eventually brought her to the hospital, Alba's mother went into hysterics at the sight of her ruined daughter. A triage nurse gave her a powerful sedative and she instantly fell asleep. The nurse found a bed for her where she slept until she awoke into the fresh nightmare of reality.

The senior officer went up to the coffee machine and slotted sixty cents into it for a macchiato. He drained his coffee swiftly, thinking of his own small family and of how he would cope with such an awful event. The case required him to exercise all his diplomacy and skill to deal with the imminent moment of the two men's meeting. He stared at Alba's face, his own leaden and hard to read. He made the decision to drop the matter of the money. In all likelihood it had been stolen, but this girl's plight had moved him. The girl's mother had been cleft in two by the tragedy. Surely now was the time for leniency.

He stepped back and stared out of the window. The sky was as blue as a bird's wing.

Mario was the first to arrive. He looked at Alba's face and all the strength drained out of his body. He slumped, but through a titanic effort of will, recovered and gritted his teeth. He approached Alba and looked at her with infinite tenderness. His face broke into discordant lines, but he would not allow himself to cry. He uttered spasmodic, incomprehensible words and bowed his head for a long time.

The police officer walked up to Mario and gently took him aside. They exchanged muted words and then a doctor told Mario that Alba's nose had been broken, her jaw had been shattered, that her ribs and right femur had been snapped, that she had sustained massive blood loss, but her condition was now stable. She would most probably require plastic surgery and her face might be forever disfigured.

Pasquale arrived and waited at the door to the room. At the sight of Mario, whose back was turned to him, he hesitated. Mario was too lost in his torment to be aware of Pasquale's presence. The officer went up to Pasquale and escorted him outside into the corridor.

'What happened?' he said in a weak voice.

'Your friend . . . had an accident . . . .'

Pasquale nodded blankly. The corridor seemed to recede into a vacuum.

'I wanted to say . . . that is to say . . . the gentleman in there . . . he doesn't know who you are, does he? Is that correct?'

'Yes.'

'So I would imagine . . . your presence here might take him by surprise?'

'Please . . . please can you let me in . . . so that I can see her?'

'Please, sir, can you try and be patient . . . if the gentleman there sees you . . . you understand . . . we don't want to make this situation more terrible than it already is.'

'My Alba, what has happened to you?'

Mario passed through into the corridor and stopped in front of Pasquale. The officer motioned as though to intervene, but his movements were uncertain.

'Who's this?' Mario demanded of the policeman.

Pasquale stared at him obliquely. He wanted to say, 'Someone who loves Alba,' but he said nothing.

The officer replied evenly, 'This gentleman is a friend of Alba's.'

'Where have I seen you before? You look familiar,' said Mario.

'It's possible.'

'I've seen you before. You were standing outside Alba's place, I am sure of it. You were holding . . .'

Mario stopped short. He studied the thin stranger in front of him. He studied the delicate, well-groomed face, the smooth hands, the expressive eyes and full lips. He wasn't quite a stranger. Not quite. Because Mario now realised that he had shared something with this person, something very precious, now damaged. He had shared Alba with him. All his limbs grew taut.

The police officer extended his hand slightly, almost as if about to shake Mario's hand. Then he murmured gently, 'Our grief must make enmity lose its venom.' Pasquale began to weep. The officer's words had finally released his sorrow.

Mario's mind filled with molten memories of Alba's sweetness and passion. Pasquale wiped away his tears. The two men looked into each other's eyes. The police officer's words and his own memories wrought a change in Mario. Now he felt only pity for the broken, stooped figure staring back at him. Alba's condition and his own despair had dissolved his world, had dissolved everything. He had nothing left. The strain of the whole situation struck them both down, and they were like two puppets whose wires have been cleanly snapped.

The officer murmured, 'Let me go and find you both some coffee,' and he left them alone together. Pasquale nodded imperceptibly. Mario said quietly, 'Sí.'

'Can I . . . do you mind if I go in and see her?' Pasquale asked.

## Alba

Mario did not stop him.

Pasquale entered the room. There she was, his angel, with all those terrible wires and tubes, her face unrecognisable, her eyes closed in a comfortless sleep, a living ghost. She couldn't see him, she couldn't touch him, she couldn't speak. In the corner, cowering under a small table, still trembling in shock and fear, was the small dog Alba had taken in. No one had noticed the poor thing. Pasquale motioned to it and in as kind a voice as he could muster tried to reassure it, but it just whimpered pitifully. But after a while Pasquale's voice seemed to calm the animal and it became still. But it would not move from its sanctuary. Pasquale was filled with unbearable pity for Alba and for the dog, for all this frightful suffering, and as his eyes took in the complicated monitors and units around Alba, he wished that he could reach her in that shadow zone she now inhabited, wished that he could reverse time, and set her free. He recalled the tenderness of their caresses, their whispered conversations in the night, in the small hours before dawn. His memories would become an antidote against loss, agonising though they were, and he promised himself that he would live through them until she recovered, and he silently prayed, no, begged for her to be all right. But reality would not capitulate and life seemed to him then like a tree stripped bare by winter, its skeletal outline starkly defined against a sequestered horizon. He searched ever and again for some semblance of colour in that place of desolation.

Pasquale turned to see Mario standing next to him and he felt Mario's arm on his shoulder. The unexpected kindness of this dismantled all his preconceptions about him and he was stirred by a deep, unknown emotion. He was about to say something when he was stopped short; for he knew that all words were as desiccated as that ravaged tree. For his part, Mario steeled himself for a long and brutal journey, whose destination was unknown. They stood there together in silence, united by grief, as the evening slowly drew in.

# THE FEVER

LIGHT, DARK, LIGHT, dark, so it goes, the same old symphony, the same old pattern. They told me to drive to the guy, the big guy, the boss, the genius, the man who pisses pink champagne, and who craps caviar. I knocked on his door in Lincoln, Nebraska, he handed me the package. This big guy, the master, he handed me the package, said to me, you'd better have AC or the trip might leave you dead, you better not lose that package or I might leave you dead, it's hot, kid, it's hot, the contents of that package are hot, I'm not talking about the sun frying your retinas, don't lose that package kid or I'll pick up your ashes and cast them into the wind, it's hot kid, what's in that package, don't blow it, don't fuck up kid, you can make it, you can do it, you can pull out all the stops, you can send the hounds packing, you can generate enough heat with that thing in your hands to launch the space shuttle.

So I took the package respectfully, handled it as though it was Scarlett Johansson's digitally remastered pussy, got back in my bruised Chrysler and began to drive like a suicidal vagrant whose ship had come in and he was being offered one last glimpse of paradise before his body expired.

I had to make it all the way to Los Angeles. The final stages of the trip involved a hypnotised spell in the Mojave Desert with its honey mesquite trees and tumbleweeds and cacti and lizards and a blowtorch sun and the unreal skies and the desolation and the cosmic American landscape. Just me, the car, the package, the bottles of Miller beside me offering to lubricate my soul, so long as no cops spotted me as I trailed a blaze of toxic speed, dust clouds blooming around my tyres, the smell of gasoline in the wind, tainting that pristine nothingness of the desert. That nothingness was perfect for me because that nothingness was my life.

The Cowboy Junkies' "Escape is so Simple" had been on repeat forever, that cool, almost imperceptible voice, that distant resignation. Pressing the gas, driving the machine hard, the wind vacuuming off the dust between the cracks, the elemental tapestries being weaved around me, and for a moment, for a second, it was perfect, the music vibrating, a low hum, the engine purring, the infinite possibilities of life spilling out of the landscape, the desert offering some nameless beauty. Consciousness seemed to expand in vibrating rings, pulsing out like the 2010 Gulf of Mexico oil spill.

The light was fading, the evening was coming. There was no stopping it. By then I'd moved on from the Cowboy Junkies to Chris Isaak by way of Johnny Cash. I glanced at the package slumped on the back seat. It was still intact. No ants had eaten into it, gaffer tape squeezed it like bandages round an Egyptian mummy.

I pulled up at a desert motel. I needed a shower, a bed, some kind of sanctuary for a few hours. Time had decomposed the place. In fact it looked like it had been abandoned years ago. Discarded branches were scattered before its entrance like cigarette butts and the wooden sign that announced it was slanted at an acute angle, hanging from a tall stump of wood, looking like it might decapitate a passing stranger. The windows were thick with grime. Despite all this the place attracted me and I pulled into the parking lot, where plastic bags stirred in the residual wind. Maybe I'd find the dregs of humanity there.

I parked with precision and care, picked up the package. It was cold to the touch, icy cold. It felt like it had just been sitting in a freezer. This was weird, given that the temperature was over a hundred. And the fact of the iciness of the package could not be explained by the car's air conditioning. I got out shakily, cradling the package and walked up to the reception. A large, bovine woman was behind the counter. She made me think of a squashed cream puff. She nodded up from her airport novel and glanced at me without a flicker of interest.

'You wan' a room?' she enquired with all the charm of an anaemic tax inspector.

'Yes.'

'You wan' a single or a double?'

'A single.'

'You got any ID?'

I produced my driver's licence.

'This do?'

'I guess so,' she said in a lazy drawl. She began to write carefully with a half-chewed ballpoint pen. I clutched the package protectively.

'You got any luggage?'

'No, that is, nothing apart from this package.'

'Mind if I ask what's inside?'

'Well, actually yes I do.'

'There's a new law around here, we've been instructed by the sheriff to ask about packages. Could be terrorism. Or could be drugs.'

'Do I look like a terrorist?'

'Maybe, maybe not.'

She reached into her handbag and pulled out a chocolate-chip cookie and began nibbling at it like a hamster.

'But I guess you look ok. But listen, mister, why don't you just tell me what's in the package and we'll leave it at that. I won't call the sheriff. You look ok.'

'It's a manuscript.'

At this point I realized that the package no longer felt so icy and cold.

'What's a manucrit?'

'It's the typewritten pages of a book, actually a novel.'

'You write it? You a writer?'

'No, it was written by someone else.'

'Who?'

'Listen lady, are you going to give me the fucking keys or what?'

'Ok, ok, take it easy, jus' doing my job, is all. That'll be twenty bucks for the room. Payment upfront. Check out 10 am.'

I gave her the money. She gave me the keys. 'Number 13, down the hall.'

I didn't know a thing about the novel. The master I mentioned at the start. It was his work. His editor was in LA, you see. So here's the scoop. This guy, this genius, this giant of literature, he's old school. He types on an old Olivetti, makes a single carbon-copy for himself when he types. He's ruled out the computer, the fax, the attachment, the email, this fucker wants his masterpiece to be handed in person to his associate as though it were an aluminium case stuffed with loot. He doesn't want to take a flight, he doesn't want to send it through the mail, he's old school, he wants it handed over in person as if it's gold bullion. No one gets to hack into his work on the internet, no spies, no voyeurs, no geeks, no nerds, no government agencies, no NSA, no CIA, no FBI, no IRS, no interception at the critical moment, no advance viewing, no Twitter, no Shitter, no Facebook, no hype, no spoiler, no press leaks, no nothing. And I'm the courier, I've been paid in spades by his publisher to drive and deliver, to be a good boy, to do as I'm told.

He is the Elvis of literature. As I said, he craps caviar and pisses pink champagne. He's as eccentric as Howard Hughes and as classic as a Ferrari. He writes prose of a beauty that makes grown men weep and women squirt. He is the Alpha and the Omega, the final word in Final Words, the Writer whose every phrase gets emblazoned onto the fabric of consciousness as surely as if it were a laser beam. This wizard, this charmer, this old-style magus doesn't sit around and wait for the Muse to descend, he doesn't chew tobacco or sip whisky and pass away an idle hour, he is a machine, a writing machine, a precision machine squeezing out masterworks like chickens lay eggs.

*The Overdog* (1986), his first novel, had been about a man who has a bizarre skin disease that targets his face which, at intervals, undergoes a complete meltdown and subsequent recreation, thus freakishly allowing him to 'become' different people, presenting in turn to the world the face of a poet, an athlete, an angel, a pugilist. His second, *Prototype of Love* (1990), was told from the point of view of a pregnant man. *The Sound of Extinction* (1995) was about meeting God, who turns out to be this little guy who goes around with a supermarket trolley. The books grew larger and more ambitious. *The Philosopher King* (2001) was set in a remote village in

Cyprus whose inhabitants were pig ignorant and primitive. Then one day a stranger takes up residence there and his exotic appearance gives rise to all sorts of rumours and the village splits into those who like him and those who don't. Gradually he takes over and sets up a kind of new society based on Ancient Athens, educates everybody, and improves life in the village until egomania takes hold and his various money-making schemes lead to disaster and the village's total destruction. Next came *The Millions* (2004), a 900-page satire about an agency in New York that specializes in faking alternate lives for people whose own lives are boring and uneventful. The agency produces documents, diplomas, certificates, letters, emails, creates an illustrious, exotic past for those who come knocking at its door. Eventually the real and the fake become indivisible as people struggle to concoct even more lies to support the original lies. The fake biographies sabotage the actual until reality itself becomes one vast and bloated invention. *The Overhaul* (2008) chronicled the decline of a wealthy American family over four generations. The narrative spanned hundreds of years, evoking in hallucinatory detail the Native American genocide, episodes from the American civil War, the assassination of Martin Luther King and the attack on the World Trade Center. What finally emerges is the complete culpability of money. The origins of the family's fortune lie in eighteenth century slavery. Key events from the twentieth century – the Vietnam War, the Indonesian killings of 1965–66, the first Gulf War – all obliquely yield immense sources of revenue for the family and the novel eventually grows into a gigantic portrait of greed and human cruelty whose final chapter shows Riley Jude Stenneford, the heir to a fortune of $80 billion, realizing that his entire identity has its roots in the evils of his forefathers and that his lifestyle, his choices, the very fabric of his being is irrevocably entwined with the real legacy of his family: money made from blood and human misery. He throws a gargantuan New Year's Eve party, the family mansion becoming a vortex of every conceivable instance of lust and decadence. After the midnight celebrations die down, he offers the surviving family members port wine of a rare vintage from a diamond-encrusted decanter. The port has been laced with strychnine and the whole clan, including Riley, goes into convulsions and asphyxiates. The book garnered tremendous critical acclaim and several death threats and there were rumours that the CIA and the FBI had subsequently opened files on him.

No one knew the subject of his latest novel. No one even knew the title.

I wrestled with the key and stepped in. I placed the package carefully on a side table and switched on the lamp. Dirty light, dirty windows. Light, dark. The place was a lousy dump. But it would do. I was exhausted. I closed the door, on the back of which a scrawled sign read KEEP DOOR CLOSED: SNAKE SPOTTED.

I stared hard at the package. What lay inside it? What gems and what pearls? Did that package somehow contain the guy? Did it contain his essence? All that was best about him? Was that package, in the final count, more real, more destined for immortality than the man himself? It had been made abundantly clear to me that on no account was I to open it. It had been made digitally clear that if that package were tampered with my balls would be neatly severed from my scrotum. I stared hard at the thing. Or maybe what lay in there was no good after all, was just scrambled shit . . .

The motel room was stuffy. I walked over and yanked open a window. This didn't really have any effect. I stared outside at nothing, at the barren night, approaching like the onset of a disease, the night of longing and sexual desire and unanswered calls for companionship. Then I took one of those interminable pisses, one of those that last so long that your legs begin to buckle and you have to prop yourself up against the wall with your arms. I pulled out a Marlboro and smoked it right down to the filter.

I walked back over to the package. It was warm. I'm not joking. The damn thing was emanating heat like a computer. What was going on with it? First it was freezing cold, now it was warm, it was as though the thing had been plugged into an electrical source. It seemed as if the package was alive, it seemed to be a living thing. I managed to foil a mad impulse to open it. I was beginning to get scared. I took the thing over to the closet and shoved it inside. I walked out into the corridor and over to my car, opened it up, pulled out the bottles of beer and returned with them and opened one up and took a long gulp. That steadied me and I spread out on the bed. The springs whined in protest. Then I finished off all the beer.

Before I knew it I was sleeping. But it was short-lived and I woke up a couple of hours later. I stared at my watch. It was 2:30 in the morning. I instinctively knew I wouldn't be able to get back to sleep. I switched on the bedside lamp and went over to the cupboard. I touched the package. It was no longer warm and no longer cold. For a moment I thought I'd imagined its altering states. But it was true, the package had been cold, had been hot. It was insane, it had been driven mad by its contents, or maybe it was a package that was subject to the freakish extremities of climate change.

As I stood there in the grip of that drenched mixture of unreality and mental depletion that accompanies a nocturnal awakening when amnesia seems to melt your brain and the events of your life are misty, I heard a tapping, from the room next to mine. It was hard to identify what was making the sound. I glanced out of the window where I found nothing but the parking lot half swallowed in the void of night. This was the desert. The desert where life existed, but barely, where the only friends to be had were the shadows, rustling like leaves and pattering like leaves on the fringes of consciousness. There was nothing here, not even a yellowing skeleton in the closet that might be dragged out and danced with in a last-ditch attempt to ward off terminal loneliness.

The next part of this whole thing is rather hard to describe. As I was sitting there, feeling myself sinking deeper and deeper, I began to have the impression that the boundaries of reality were being redrawn, that they were shifting, that a seismic shift was taking place and that my motel room was no longer a motel room, but more like a chamber passing through space.

I kept on staring out of the window. I turned away but, when I turned back again, at once – with the awful certainty that accompanies dread – I knew that something was wrong. I looked through the murky window. A tall, dark figure with his back to me, standing motionless and inert. He just stood there, looking out into space, wrapped up in a brown raincoat. What the hell was he doing out there in the dead of night? I watched, the curtain pulled towards me to conceal my presence. It might have been a statue as opposed to an actual human being. As I looked I began to feel my throat growing dry. I needed water, and with two long strides made it to the bathroom. I let the faucet run and downed a glass. When I got back to the window, he, it, was still there. I just couldn't take my eyes away from him. Indivisible horror was rising, spinning its sticky web. I was aware of my hands tightening into fists. It was as though the weight of what I saw was pushing against, crushing, my ability to interpret it. I was seized with the idea that if I could just catch a glimpse of its face my curiosity would be laid to rest, so I decided to venture out there, leave my safe room and stare the thing in the eyes. I could feel my heart vaulting as I hurried down the corridor, and my legs seemed to have turned to jelly. But I came out into the parking lot where tumbleweeds were rocking hypnotically in the residual wind and there he was again, carved out of wood, in the distance, and I could tell then that he was not of this world, that he was tangible and three dimensional and at the same time made out of shadows, as though countless shadows had meshed themselves together in such a way as to form matter, but I was so unnerved that I couldn't take another step and I just stood there too, a counterpart of percolating impressions, uncertainties, and I was aware of the silence, the punctured plastic bags that stirred imperceptibly, beautifully, the motel sign, which, in that remote tenebrosity, took on the angular dimensions of a gigantic tombstone, the dead branches about me, like splintered fragments of a raft in a salt dead sea, the sea about me that was the desert, where everything was etched and unreal as the sky hung heavy with blackness and the dying world, and then the figure turned and turned in such a way as to exactly meet my gaze and I could see that where his forehead and temples should have been there were just vast black cavities, gigantic holes, and I began to scream, I began to scream and then it seemed to me that all my blood was being syphoned out of my veins and arteries and my body was being shut down and I ran back into the motel, everything breaking up, my vision growing dim, my mind coming apart at the seams, as I panted and dived back into the motel, slamming the entrance door, locking it frantically, and the dim light of the corridor was strange, foggy, as I stood outside my room, trembling and heaving, my first thought to drive the hell out of there, despite my fear, my exhaustion, the blackness of the night. As I grappled with my keys, another door, way down the corridor, on the opposite side to my room, opened slowly. A woman stepped out uncertainly. She had blonde hair. She wore blue jeans. She could see that I was too scared to pose any danger to her. She weighed up the situation, probably assuming from my behaviour that I was either mad or sick.

'I – I'm sorry, I didn't mean to scream – there's – there's something in the parking lot . . .'

'Jesus, are you ok?' She spoke with a strong Alabama twang.

'There's . . . there's something out there. It was . . . it was standing right outside my room . . . I can't go back inside there . . . I just can't . . .'

'Oh my lord. Are you ok?' She inched up to me. She was on the wrong side of forty, with depleted features and a beaten-up body, but not unattractive, not without a certain 3am allure. She was wearing a blue denim shirt and she was smoking a cigarette.

'I can't go back inside my room. I just . . . can't . . . it was out there . . . in the lot . . .' I stammered.

She watched me as I unravelled before her, and something held her to me. She had latched on to my torment.

'Listen. Honey. What do you say we fix you a drink? I've got some bourbon. How does that sound? In my room? You sure look like you could use a stiff one.'

'Yes, that . . . sounds good.'

'You ok with that plan?'

I nodded slowly. Some strength returned to my frazzled legs.

'That's what I thought, we can fix you a little drink and we can have a little chat and you can tell me what you saw. That way you'll be safe. In my room. Safe and cosy. But you're ok, aren't you? You're not dangerous or anything? You're a gentleman, right?'

'Yes . . . of course.'

'I thought so, but, you know, thought I'd ask, just the same.'

I looked into her eyes, they were large and mild and blue and her self-possession acted on me like Xanax and I followed her, docile, into her room. There was an overpowering smell of cheap perfume and on the little table next to her bed were two cracked glasses and a bottle of bourbon, almost as if she'd been expecting me.

'You feelin' a lil' better, treasure?'

I nodded. She poured a drink and handed it to me.

I managed a smile and I could see that she was the kind of person who didn't need things to be spelled out, she was easy going and had been through more than her fair share of shit and had emerged with a crust of unflappability. I took a sip of bourbon and felt it erupt in my throat. I was with another human being, a desirable woman, I had company,

I had alcohol. The night no longer seemed nightmarish, interminable.

'What was it that you thought you saw? Whatever it was had you all shook up pretty damned good.'

'I don't know, I don't know. Do you mind if we don't talk about it?'

'No, I don't mind. Don't mind at all.'

Exhaustion knocked me sideways like a freight train. The madness of the last few minutes shredded my inhibitions and I just blurted out what was on my mind, 'Listen, this might sound crazy, but do you mind if I sleep in your bed, with you tonight, I just don't think I can sleep in that room, knowing . . . knowing . . . that it's . . . that . . .'

She looked urgent with curiosity. I said nothing. She said nothing. I took another sip of bourbon.

'Sure, you can sleep in my bed. Actually it'll be kind of nice to have a man in bed, kind of nice to have someone to snuggle up to. Haven't had a man in my bed . . . since . . . oh, how long's it been now? How long since I left Ray? Well, you aren't interested in my lil' old life, are you now? Tell the truth, I'm much more interested in you and what it was that spooked you so much. Only, you said you didn't want to talk about it, so that's fine by me, fine by me, but I must say, you've kind of got me hooked.'

'Was Ray your husband?'

'Yeah, that's right, that good for nothing piece of shit was my husband, 'till I kicked him out and he wasn't my husband no more. Yeah he was as low as they get, old Ray, yes siree, a real piece of shit, a real evil motherfucker.'

'What did he do? To you?'

'Well . . . if you really wanna know . . . well . . . it's kind of upsetting . . . and . . . seeing as I don't know you, and all . . .' She paused, seemed to reconsider, then started again, with renewed vigour, 'He used to beat me 'till I was black and blue . . . he was . . . a thief, a liar . . . he was violent, dumb, zero personal hygiene . . . and he fucked around . . . hell, he even fucked my kid sister . . . guess it served me right for being so trusting . . . but . . . well . . . he's probably in some gutter now somewhere . . . holding his dick in his hand . . . not a dime to his name . . . like a . . . like a big fat drunken fart. I'm just too goddamn nice, that's me, too trusting, too nice. I think I got a sign tattooed on my head saying, "Walk right all over me." What do you think? Did I give off that vibe?'

'No. You seem pretty tough. Pretty tough. And you were very kind just now. Not many people would have given me the time of day. I must have struck you as crazy. I'm ok now, but . . . back then, wow, I was . . . you must have thought . . . I was a real nut case.'

'Well, you did seem to be a bit . . . you were definitely acting . . . like . . . you were shook up all right. But actually, I been around a lot of crazy people . . . I used to work in a mental institution . . . sometimes the patients would throw tantrums . . . try and slit their wrists, you know, it wasn't very easy . . . it was actually pretty tiring . . . but, it's like anything else . . . after a while you get used to it . . . it becomes normal.'

As she talked I began to ask myself if I was actually insane. Had I finally gone insane? Had it been the driving? Was it the manuscript? My nothing life?

'Listen, honey, I hate to be the one to say it, but I'm kinda beat. I don't mind you sleeping with me, in my bed – but no funny business – but right now I think we should both hit the sack, it's late and I gotta get up early 'cause I'm headed north, all the way up to Spokane.'

'Sure.'

'Where you headed, darlin'?'

'South, Los Angeles.'

I stared again into her blue eyes. In that instant a connection was made and I was filled with tenderness for this complete stranger. We took off our clothes, leaving our underwear, and climbed into the bed and it was all very natural. She cuddled up to me and whispered in my ear, 'How does that feel?'

'It's .... nice. I feel safe. Cosy.'

I placed my hand against the base of her neck. She didn't object. I began to stroke her hair very very softly. She stretched her arm out and switched off the bedside lamp. We lay there together in the dark. I felt suspended between grief and joy. Part of me wanted to kiss her, but it seemed to me, laying there, in the motel, in darkness, that a kiss would only chalk up pain later, that each kiss would add to the pain tapestry, would be another stitch and bit of embroidery in the pain tapestry so I resisted and I guess she resisted too.

Sleep rolled over me like a great tidal wave.

I was awake again. Something was happening. My eyes opened, my body contorted, the darkness was everywhere, but I felt super attenuated pleasure in my loins, surging, coruscating through me, and then I knew, with a kind of unsettling joy, that she had taken my penis in her mouth and it felt like the palpitations of her lips and tongue were loosening the nuts and bolts of my brain until it was firing and glittering like phosphorescent confetti twisting in the column of a tornado. I heard her husky, nocturnal voice murmur, 'That nice? Darlin'?' The words sounded alien and unreal. I was aware of my body acquiescing to its own exquisite sacrifice. I felt my core, my essence being re-written, the contours of my personality changing, I already knew that this moment, these moments were signalling my transit into a foreign land, that I was passing through the borders, and from now I would be an exile in my own life, later to be deprived of this fatal intoxication, searching in vain for it. As she impelled me, tenderly, firmly, and, in the end, frantically towards orgasm, my molecules broke apart, the barrier between my physical self and the universe dissolved, my brain became vapour and I slumped into a place of crystalline oblivion, expunged of words, of thoughts, practically of consciousness.

Very very slowly, the world began to creep back in. My singed and scorched limbs gradually became capable again of movement. In the darkness I could hear her breathing fast. She whispered, her voice golden, 'Darlin', I feel . . . wasn't that, wasn't that just somethin' . . . ? You taste very sweet, like milk and honey, darlin', I kind of feel you still on my lips, my tongue, in my mouth, you've done something to me. You've turned on a switch inside me. I never knew it could be like that. You're so different from Ray, so . . . so different.'

I didn't know what to say. I could see light coming in at the edges of the curtains. The night was expiring. I thought of the drive waiting for me. I wondered again about what it was that I'd seen before: those terrible black cavities.

'I don't know your name, I just realised,' I whispered.

'Likewise. Let's not bother with our names. Maybe it's better that way. Soon I'll have to get going, day's breaking. I

## The Fever

got to drive to Spokane. Too bad you aren't headed the same way.... Now that I've met you, I'd kind of like to stay with you in this bed, not move for a day or two. You know what I mean?' She laughed easily.

'Yeah, I know what you mean.'

A blade of light sliced across the room, a thin corridor of light. It caught her features. She was on the verge of tears.

'I have to tell you something. I need to tell you something.'

I was silent. Then I said, 'Go ahead.' The world outside was coming into focus again, the sun was rising, the earth preparing itself for another day. Today people around the world would go to work, have lunch, fall in love, kill one another for the sake of greed, for the sake of love, people would smoke cigarettes and inject heroin, would make porn films and surf the internet, people would commit suicide and get married, would bury loved ones and drink toasts. All of this would happen today.

'I killed Ray. I killed him. With my gun. Shot him twice in the head. Believe me, he deserved it. If anyone did, he did. No doubt about that. And you know what? I think I did the right thing. Maybe they'll catch me in the end. Probably. But I just had to do it. I had to rid the world of Ray. Just to make the world that tiny bit better, ya know?

'Do you think I'm out of my goddamn mind?'

I didn't say anything. What could I say? Did I think she was mad? I guess so. I guess murder is madness. In a flash I understood. Understood what it was I'd seen.

'You're probably no madder than the average person, I'd say.'

She turned over to me and in the sunlight her eyes attained an incredible pitch of luminosity.

'Thank you for saying that. You're a sweet guy. Too sweet for most women, I expect, too sweet. Stupid dumb bitches don't know what they're missing. But that's the way the cookie crumbles.'

I stared at her, trying to disguise my uneasiness. She had killed a man. The last twelve hours had been so strange. I realized then that I had to get out of there. Had to leave this woman, this murderess's bed. It wasn't anything to do with fear, but I no longer felt I could deal with being so close to her. Too much proximity, too much intimacy, too much something.

'I should get going,' I said, my voice cracking.

She smiled and I could see that her eyes were welling up with tears, though none actually fell.

'I guess I scared you?'

'No. Not really.'

She adjusted her hair, smoothed it down. As if she were getting ready to go out. Then she reached over and poured herself a slug of bourbon and downed it.

'Thank you for listening. I needed to tell someone. I really, really needed to tell someone. I feel a lot better now.'

I leaned over and kissed her softly on the lips. Then I got out of bed. The room was filling with more and more light. Intense, distilled light. She watched me with a kind of finishing-line tenderness.

I didn't want to say goodbye, it seemed so final. I just smiled and left, as noiselessly as I could.

I closed the door to her room. As I did so I realized that she was already slipping into the nebulous realm of memory.

I walked a little shakily to room 13 and unlocked the door

and sat down on the bed. I didn't know if I had the energy for the rest of the drive. I stared at the nightstand. I opened it. The package sat there, ugly and squat and dull. What was I doing with my life? What kind of life was it? At once, without hesitation, I started opening the package, ripping away the black tape that carefully sealed it. I pulled out the manuscript. The typewritten paper was burningly hot under the touch of my fingers. At once the paper ignited in orange and red flames and a foul, metallic odour was released into the air and then the pages underneath were claimed in the flames and I dropped the whole thing as it became an inferno spreading with unstoppable speed, and by the time I had reached the bathroom to get some water, the fire had spread to the nightstand which, after a brief resistance, also became an orange blur. The sunlight was streaming brilliantly into the room; the day outside was fully formed, bursting with promise and beauty and mystery. I stared out of the window, into the parking lot and made out my trusted Chrysler. No one, nothing, was out there. Neither ghosts nor predators. I looked back at the fire, now happily claiming the rest of the room, generating stupendous heat, turning my humble motel room into the greatest show on earth, a spectacle as awe-inspiring as anything that the master had yet dreamed up. I continued to stare into those fluctuating, purifying flames. And I knew that it was all right. It was all going to be all right in the end.

# THE OPIATE EYES
# OF THE BUDDHA

I

THE BEACH WAS deserted, and the only thing that might have indicated the presence of civilisation was a skeletal fishing boat that stood like a gigantic misshapen bone in the sand. Beyond stretched a line of palm trees in a gracious arc, and beyond them there was only sky. Here it was perpetual summer.

Two young women were swimming far out. Their heads rose above the swell of the sea, which was pulsing with untamed energy. Gradually they began to make their way back towards land. Both were excellent swimmers, so they knew how to harness the power of the waves rather than be hindered by them. They emerged, slender, glowing figures in the early morning light, and flopped onto their towels, which they had laid out beside their rucksacks. They didn't speak and there was a sense that they were bound by some unspoken rule that dictated silence. One of the women searched inside her rucksack and pulled out a banana, which she peeled quickly, and passed a piece to the other, who took it without a word, conveying her thanks with a quick smile. The latter pulled out a cowboy hat and set it squarely on her head, and the waves of her strawberry blond hair were tamed by its presence into something less unruly. Then she lit a cigarette and inhaled;

the smoke poured out in an elegant whirl. Her companion turned to her and seemed to be taking her to task for smoking; her eyes were at once severe and mocking. They both stared at the ocean, which pulsed with tireless, perpetual motion. It was like the most perfect machine that had ever been constructed, never breaking down, never aging, and requiring neither fuel nor supervision for its smooth running. They stared for a little while more before the sun's glare became too intense and they closed their eyes and rested. The girl with the hat stubbed her cigarette out on a piece of cardboard that she carried everywhere in order to record the number of cigarettes she had smoked. She placed both the butt and the cardboard in a small transparent plastic bag. Then she pulled out a battered book entitled *Mysteries of the Cosmos* and slid it under her head in the manner of a makeshift pillow.

Overhead the sun was attaining its maximum intensity and clouds were jerked asunder and dispelled in its orbit. The girl in the cowboy hat was reminded of little ants running away from the flame of a lighter. She reached out for her sun block and started applying it to her legs and stomach with subtle, circular movements. Her companion signalled for her to pass the cream, but she steadfastly refused to and pursed her lips insolently.

'Katherine, please, let me have some of that sun stuff.'

'All good things come to those who wait,' Katherine replied.

Then, when she had finally extracted as much as she needed from the orange tube, she passed it over.

'Thank you, your highness. Did anyone ever tell you you are a princess? A spoiled princess?'

'Many people told me I was a princess, and one person once told me that I was a princess who came from another, higher planet and had been forced to settle for this one for a while.'

'That pretty much says it all.'

Katherine reached out to stroke her companion's hair, which, like her own, was strawberry blond, but reached down to her last vertebra and was now concealed behind her back, pressed between it and her beach towel.

'Katherine, where did you get that cowboy hat?'

'Don't you remember? I picked it up in Unawatuna, in that little shop with the scarves and sarongs. The guy was so nice, he had such a cool nose stud, diamond-fantastic. Don't tell me you don't remember, Katya?'

'My brain's fried from all the sun and moving around. And I'm still jet lagged.'

'Christy mercy. That's hard. Somehow I shook off the plane pretty quick. Must be my biorhythms or melatonin or some such thing.'

'It's wonderful here, isn't it?'

'It's ok.'

'Ok? Is that it?'

'Ok is a lot in my book. Ok is the highest possible praise.'

She rolled onto her stomach and her supple, brown back caught Katja's attention. Katherine's tan was even and full and her body glowed with health. For a moment Katja envied her, her easy grace and confidence. Katja glanced down at her own calves and arms, pale and slightly chubby.

'Actually,' Katherine began, 'I find it a bit . . . I don't know . . . scary here. No, not scary. That's not the right word. It's more sad.'

'Sad? All this beauty? Really?'

'There's a sadness about this beach. Ok, it's beautiful, we

get that it's beautiful. But it's crying out for some humanity to come and fill it, for some chaos and noise and a few beach bars and some hot dog stands and a couple of surfers. I don't know. Or a few reindeers and mistletoe or something. After all, it is Christmas time, hard as that might be to imagine in all this unsnowiness.'

'Why would you want to ruin it with all that garbage? It's perfect as it is. And since when did you care about Christmas? This is perfection, or as near as damn it.'

'Yeah, maybe, but it fills me with sadness and with fear. The beauty I see here is like the beauty of some virginal young girl who has never left her bedroom and will never make love. And she'll just stay trapped there in her beautiful bubble with her beautiful trinkets and jewels but no one will ever get to see her wear them. It's so sad this place. Let's go.'

'I don't understand you, this is the kind of place most people dream of. This is the kind of beach that hasn't been ruined by commercialism yet, it's still undiscovered, a secret.'

'I can't explain it, I just feel this immense sadness and something else.'

'What?'

'Something like nausea.'

'Oh Christ.'

'It feels like this place is cursed to me, like there's this toxic energy emanating from here. An evil force. Maybe it's the legacy of the famous tsunami.'

'You know, sometimes I wish I had a less complicated sister. It can be exhausting to have to deal with all your flights of fancy.'

'I know, I know. It's exhausting for me too, being me. I wish I was less sensitive to every mood, feeling, I wish I could just switch off my brain sometimes or slip into a coma for a while. Better still, spend a year dead. I just can't seem to bear this sense that I am me all the time, that I have to always be me, that I am always stuck in this body, this mind, these limbs, this skin. Sometimes I think that being myself means having to watch television all the time. Being myself is like a television that I can't turn off. I can't leave this house, this place, my body, and it's like I'm barricaded in myself. I've been myself for a lifetime. You know what I mean? Maybe I'm like that beautiful princess – maybe this beach makes me sad because it forces me to confront myself. There's no place to hide. You know me, I'm always looking for the next fix, the next drug, the next distraction.'

Katja studied her sister's face, trying to work out how serious she was being. She knew that Katherine tended to express deep things in a playful way.

Katherine stared at the sea, searching for a pattern or formula in its ever-changing configurations that would unlock its ultimate meaning.

'Doesn't it make you nervous, being here, so close to where the tsunami happened?' she asked.

Katja made no reply. There was a silence trying to emerge, but it was always stymied by the angry crashing tide. Seconds moved past sluggishly, time slowed to a pulsation that held the potential for a thousand tragic abortions and eruptions; the natural world split into two parts: the serene, sublime canvas that they saw, and the undiluted terror behind it, which would accompany the destruction of life once that canvas was ripped and torn down in the split seconds of calamity. At every moment, every instant, Katherine was suffocatingly aware of the possibility that something could happen, a disaster unfold, and that knowledge weighed her down, quickened her breathing, and pulled her eyes back in vigilance.

'I mean, it gives me the creeps. It's like I look at the sea, and instead of seeing the sea, this big flat slice of water and blue, I see fear, I see death waiting to flood in. As though at any moment it might happen again. This wave from hell could blow up out of nowhere. *Capito?*'

'You know, you should write them down, all the things you say. They are diamond brilliant. You're this genius waiting to be discovered.'

'Genius, smenius. I'm just peddling words, like a drug-pusher peddles drugs. I would have been an excellent drug dealer and even better whore, lying on my back all day.'

'Hey, don't talk like that, I don't like to think of you in that way.'

'Let's make tracks, sweetie. The sun's doing my head in, I need a bit of shade. Let's walk down to the road and find a tuk-tuk and head down to Tangalle. We could check in to a cool bay hotel, what do you think?'

'Are you insane? Do you know how much those places cost?'

'Listen, I can put it on my credit card. You know the score, I chalk up the bill, Maury cuts it down to size again.'

'Your sugar daddy.'

'No, my sugar-cane daddy. My director of finances, to be exact. Maury's always bailing me out, fixing the leaks in the plumbing, pouring money into the bank, cooking the books. Maury is dependable, rational, evidence of order in the cosmos. Or at least evidence of liquidity. What would I do without him? He's my mysterious patron and ethereal ATM, lighting up like a strobe when all else fails. I feel like a rat for using him but he's saintly and kind and wants to be used.'

'And in return you offer him sexual favours?'

'Nothing so distinct. I just spend time with him. He hasn't made any formal declarations of sexual intent, he just wants to look out for me. He knows the laws of the jungle like the back of his hand, and he's anxious to shelter and nurture us, and he can afford to it in style, big sis, given that he works for a company that pays him pots of money in return for forfeiting what remains of his soul.'

They laughed.

'Let's have a Mojito,' said Katherine.

'At nine in the morning?'

'You need to live a little more.'

'I know, I know, I'm the dull, conservative one, and you're the free spirit. God, how ghastly.'

Katherine smiled in that way she did, her lips circling the length of her face with conspiratorial nonchalance. She reached out her hand and touched her sister's reassuringly. They stood up and gathered their things together and began to walk towards the trees that circled the beach in verdant, fabulous abundance. Soon they were cutting a path through the great plants, leaves swaying and trembling in the breeze. They came to a mud road and began to walk down it, careful to avoid the holes and puddles of water rapidly shrinking in the sunlight. Lizards darted about like scaled down dinosaurs. They could see an old man in a loin cloth approaching. They caught sight of his blood-red tongue as he smiled inoffensively at them. They smiled back and he bowed his head graciously. From his pocket he produced a small banana and offered it to Katja and she also bowed her head in gratitude and placed the fruit in her rucksack. The old man clapped his hands noiselessly and beamed with pleasure.

Katja said, 'Diamond-brilliant.'

Katherine said, 'Diamond-fantastic.'

The girls waved goodbye and went on. After an hour or so of hard walking they came to a main road, whose lanes were occupied by slow moving oxen and bicycles and buses blaring on their horns to alert the other drivers to their lumbering presence. They spotted and hailed a tuk-tuk – a small, three wheeled taxi that was like a scooter that had mutated into something larger, with a black canvas roof with drop-down sides. The driver immediately began to negotiate his price. After they had agreed to his terms they bundled in and stuffed their rucksacks into a small corner and sat down on the cramped back seat. As they plodded along, Katherine caught sight of an immense standing Buddha in an opening between the ubiquitous trees, his opiate eyes staring at her inscrutably. She took a photo, prompting their driver to observe sweetly, 'That statue is two hundred metres tall, madam.'

'Wow.'

'When tsunami come, water level with Buddha's head.'

'Are you a Buddhist?' Katherine asked him.

'Yes, madam.'

'Can I ask you a question?'

'Of course.'

'Why are Sri Lankans so kind? Is it because they are Buddhists?'

'I not know, madam. Perhaps. Because Buddhist they believe your actions in this life are deciding your next life, so we try to be good, try to be kind, so in next life we do not return in bad form, as elephant or as donkey.'

'So that philosophy helps you?'

'Yes, because Buddha is teaching that all deeds, all bad things done by someone are returning to harm the people who does bad. So you see, we are knowing, is not just a moment, a small thing, but we are thinking of the whole of effect, across time, across space. If you like I take you to the rock temple, near here. There you can see the Buddha inside. Very beautiful. Very high, you walk, you see all of nature. Inside there are four sleeping buddhas. We can go, you enjoy very much.'

'Perhaps, yes.'

Katja produced some raisin buns and offered one to the driver who accepted it gleefully. They all began to nibble at them. 'Can we just stop a minute? I'd like to take some more photos. Can we turn into that paddy field?' said Katherine. The driver nodded easily and they rolled towards the paddy field, brimming with water. They caught sight of a small procession heading towards them, following a path that cut through the super abundant vegetation. The sudden silence that emerged as the tuk-tuk spluttered to a halt, away from the noisy road, brought the scene before them into magical focus. A newly married couple – the bridegroom in a black suit, his luxuriant hair slicked back so that it seemed to take on the texture of blackberry jam, and his bride, bedecked in red jewels and a red nose stud and a red dress – were balanced together on an old, barely functioning bicycle. Accompanying them were a dozen smiling wedding guests. The sisters waved at this eccentric yet extraordinarily elegant group and Katherine decided to approach the couple and offer them a bun, despite Katja's initial reluctance. They accepted it, laughing; the bridegroom broke the bun into two pieces and offered half to his new wife and they ate it together. As Katherine watched them, she was suddenly seized with an emancipating love for these people whose language she didn't speak and whose beliefs she didn't share. It was faintly momentous. She turned to Katja and whispered, 'What a beautiful couple. They've singlehandedly managed to make marriage romantic again.' In the end, somewhat reluctantly, the sisters said goodbye to the wedding party and walked back to their driver. They climbed back in, only then realising that it had been foolish to leave all their things there, but their fears were instantly scattered by his aura of benevolence.

After half an hour of hard driving they came within sight of Tangalle, and the driver deposited them at the Jetwing Hotel. Katherine spoke easily with the young receptionist as the driver waited for them outside. When they learnt that the hotel had space, even though it was Christmas Eve, they paid the driver and gave him a hefty tip, which at first he refused. But on the girls' insistence he eventually accepted the money, placing his hands together in a supplicatory, endearing gesture. As he yanked on the ignition lever, he turned to them and said, 'Don't lose your smiles. Goodbye.' They watched him wistfully as he drove off, then they deposited their luggage with an old porter with many teeth missing – when he opened his mouth it was like catching sight of an old castle with its battlements cast in shadow.

Katherine had noticed the hotel's luxurious infinity pool and she was itching to take a swim, but Katja wanted to rest. They signed the register, smiled at the receptionist, and entered their room, which had a spacious balcony that looked out onto the sea and a small enclave of rocks and curving palm trees. They both flopped onto the bed.

'Gosh, the lap of luxury,' said Katja and she started taking off her clothes. 'And what a view!'

Katherine got up and went out onto the terrace, to monitor the sea and make sure it was behaving itself.

'This view is to die for,' said Katherine. 'I wish we could stay here forever. We could grow old here and be these famous eccentric old ladies who have spent their entire lives at this hotel. Eating, sleeping, drinking, writing, swimming. Now, that would be a good life. Earlier, with the honeymooners, wasn't it . . . wasn't it great?'

'Very.'

'I had this . . . I had this feeling . . . Maybe I'm starting to enjoy life after all. Maybe we aren't all just pieces of seaweed floating through the mechanistic, unfeeling universe. Maybe there is something more. Or maybe not . . . . Take a look at this view Kat. It's . . . there are no words.'

'I need to rest a bit. I think I ate too much dahl for breakfast.'

Katherine took off her cowboy hat and smiled, showing pearly white teeth. She lit a cigarette and said, practically singing: 'I can't find anything real to grasp onto. No, no, no, ha ha ha.'

'It just takes a bit of chicken soup. We'll do it a little later. Now I have to rest, sis.'

'Yes, I understand, but you know what? You're right. I reduce everything. I shouldn't. Do you remember when we went to that temple in Matara? When you gave your white teddy bear to that little girl?'

'Of course I remember. How could I forget? It was . . . magical.'

They had ventured into a Buddhist temple to light candles, which had to be bathed in coconut oil in order for their wicks to burn properly. Katja had brought along the white teddy bear, determined to give it away to a child, a child who had probably never had a real toy of her own. As they stood there, watching the locals who seemed to be lost in prayer and meditation, an old Sri Lankan lady touched Katja lightly on the elbow and showed her how to light the candle. They were beside a colossal sleeping Buddha in the *parinirvana* position, whose eyes were half closed and whose vertical, slotted-together feet were as tall as a man. Katja was about to give her a few rupees by way of thanks, but the Sri Lankan lady very gently shook her head and declined the offer. Then she rejoined her party – three other ladies and a small girl, perhaps four years old. Katja took one look at the child, with her huge brown eyes and jet black, silky curls and very quietly approached this beatific and barefoot group. Katherine watched at a distance, her camera at the ready as ever. Katja, clutching the teddy bear, careful to jettison any possible trace of hostility, reached out to the child and gave her the toy, which she immediately and smilingly accepted. As the child held onto the white form that was half her size – exuding a sense that she did not know how to hold the toy, as though each and every different thing in life needed to be held in a slightly different way, and she hadn't yet learnt the specific way of holding a teddy bear – the gathered party of ladies and the little girl tapped into some inexhaustible wellspring of joy, and they were transfigured by happiness which leapt out and enveloped the two sisters in its ethereal glow. Katherine abandoned her idea of taking a photo – to have done so at such a moment would have been odious.

'Yes, magical,' Katherine sighed. 'But can you imagine trying to explain that moment to someone in New York? Or in London? They wouldn't get it. They'd just think you were out to lunch . . . a measly one.'

She puffed on her cigarette and twirled with the smoke. Katja watched the lines of smoke as they vanished.

'Yes, they wouldn't get it,' said Katja. 'Though they might get it, if it was a commercial, or had a price tag, or was in the Tate as a bit of video art. But they – we – people – we're beginning not to get real life anymore. We don't get real life anymore. Know what I mean, Katherine?'

'You bet your bottom dollar, pound and Turkish lira I do.'

Katherine was at once energized by a new force, an unruly current that pulsed through her limbs, made her buoyant and supreme. She walked out onto the balcony and when she spoke something faintly theatrical accentuated her words.

'Ok, so let's do a little settling up. A little summation. So – we exist. The universe exists. Life evolved. Human beings evolved. A super sophisticated, super refined machine with a soul. So there we have it. We come from stardust, we go back to it. We eat, we shit, we fuck, we die. Eating and fucking are the best bits – by popular agreement. Allow me to encompass a human life. In this life, if you are lucky, you are not born in a dictatorship, or where there's disease and poverty. You have a reasonable face, a functioning brain. You don't need a sex change. You are not a hermaphrodite. You possess the correct number of limbs. You get access to an education. You get a pretty good career going and it's all going swimmingly. You are lucky cause you don't need to work in a sweat shop for Nike or Gap or Benetton, you don't have to have your face burnt off by acid courtesy of some disgruntled Middle Eastern nutcase husband with Allah or Mohammed on his side. And then – well, it's all going swimmingly, or is it?, you start to get older, fatter, you start to lose your looks, but you've got two brats to show for it. The blood pressure's rising, so is the cholesterol. It's downhill from hereon in. Insomnia, depression, emptiness. Kids flee the nest. You scramble around for a bit of meaning. You try yoga, you buy Echart Tolle, you get into DIY and watercolours. You try and pierce your nipple but it's too painful. You sponsor a child, you internet date. You finally try anal sex. But it's the old slippery slope, the old slippery slope . . . . And then . . . you decide to travel to Sri Lanka . . . and you get a room . . . in this hotel . . . and you look at this view . . . and you think . . . here I am . . . and this view is so perfect, so wonderful, so sublime that it makes you believe in something greater than yourself. The old ineffable. But is that enough? Is that enough, that's my question? That is the question, my old Kat.'

'You think too much. You have to learn to switch off your brain. You make it sound . . . you make it all sound so . . . so functional, so dry and lifeless. Get over yourself.'

'I just want . . . I just need . . . I just need to know that the universe has some form, some order, isn't just this cold place.'

'It isn't. Look around you, look at the Sri Lankans with their smiles and their kindness. Isn't that enough for you? Doesn't that give you comfort?'

'It does, yeah, I guess. But it doesn't beat a Mojito.'

'Not for me. Let's order a bit of rice and something.'

'Didn't you say that you had eaten too much dahl?'

'But now I'm hungry again – all your ruminations, speeches, sophistry, they make my brain bloated and my tummy needy.'

'So call room service, we may as well go the whole hog.'

Katja flipped over and grabbed the phone, but after stabbing a few buttons she realised it didn't appear to be working.

Then, as though something had divined her need, the phone started ringing and a melodious and slightly comical voice sounded from the other end and asked if everything was all right. Katja asked if they could order some rice and curry and then she put the receiver down, slightly bemused and puzzled.

'How did that just happen? No phone, no line, and then they call back. It's like they are all clairvoyants in this place, like they are keeping tabs on us, like they know what we are going to do before we know ourselves.'

'Yeah, I know what you mean. I think they all speak among themselves and news of our presence oscillates through the Sri Lankan universe like particles hitting the screen in the "double-slit experiment", and before you know it we are making wave patterns and are in two places at once. Or they are in two places at once waiting to serve us, pick us up and eject us. Like that time we were at the retreat at Unawatuna and we asked the receptionist how long it took to get to Galle and he tells us, and the next thing you know this disco tuk-tuk driver with the fake Bose speakers and the Big in Japan gig is waiting for us down the lane, and just happens to bow his head in our direction and say, "Madam, you looking for to go to Galle, I give good price." They are all in it together. Sometimes I feel like I'm in that show *The Prisoner*. Be seeing you!'

'Half the time I don't have the foggiest clue what you're yapping on about, but I just sit and smile politely, just to humour you, darling.'

'Diamond-brilliant. But can you imagine what will happen to this place once they discover all of the sick oil slick of surveillance. It will be murder. Or maybe once all the gizmos and cameras and gunk arrive fully fledged they'll all collectively decide to do away with it, or ignore it or chuck it all on a bonfire to Buddha and realise that they are all better off with their sixth senses and hawk's eyes and big nostrils and supernatural eyesight. And another form of chaos will just slip into place and mutate and take over. Like someone handed you two screwdrivers and instead of screwing screws with them you end up using them as chopsticks. Or someone gives you a sarong and instead of wearing it you drape it over a sofa. Or they will dispense with all the tools just like they dispense with everything except the horn when they drive. Or they'll take the closed-circuit tellies and try to watch cricket on them, or the latest Bollywood betabuster. But then they'll realise it has no signal and chuck it in the ocean with a few hoppers by way of funeral arrangements.'

Katja walked across and stepped onto the balcony – and something about the way she moved conveyed inquisitiveness and resignation at the same time. She loved the fact that her sister's brilliance was wrapped in a cocoon of the urbane and the cynical. She was like a flower that bloomed at the oddest times. Together they lapsed into silence and watched the view. They waited. They watched the sky as it heaved and convulsed with cosmic delirium. When their lunch arrived it was completely forgotten as the cinema screen before them held them and the day slowed to an inertia that was nonetheless life lived to the full, and they were like two sailors on a raft adrift in a slumberous ocean where dazzling vistas of time competed with half-glimpsed sights of the stars and the arc of the sky and they briefly and ravishingly connected to a life of sensory acuteness which left the West and all its screaming materialism far behind.

Later, as the evening came, the round dome of the sun attained a perfect symmetry of form and intensity of even burnished colour before dipping with deceptive speed into the horizon. And then it was merely a thin sliver of orange peering out above the horizontal boundary. A second later it was gone, and shortly afterwards the sky commenced its paean to its departure and bars of purple appeared until at last the whole sky became a pinkish red membrane that announced, to whoever cared to listen, the death knell of insignificance.

## 2

While Katja was having a nap, Katherine ambled down a spiral staircase and ventured outside to the deserted and enormous infinity pool. It was a field of deep resplendent blue that tapered off and curved at the far end so that the edge of the pool and the horizon of the ocean's black line appeared to join seamlessly. This created a dizzying effect and as Katherine slowly swam towards the far end and this line of welded-together blue and black drew nearer, she had the impression she was moving not towards the end of the pool, but towards the edge of the world. Far off, behind her, a palm tree swayed in the wind. The ocean's perpetual music sounded tirelessly. The haunting motion of the tree, her own motion, what her eyes saw, and the water's sensual embrace induced a kind of intoxication and she felt herself slipping into a trance whose suspension of will was matched by the slow suspension of her body after her movements had slowed, then stopped altogether.

Finally she emerged from the water and dried herself carefully. She was startled to find that she was being observed by a Sri Lankan man from a distance. As she wrapped herself up in her towel and slipped through the glass doors of the hotel, she could feel his eyes on her back, unravelling her composure. She fled up the spiral staircase. Once at the top she peered back down. But he had gone.

Upstairs, she found that a Christmas Eve party was in full swing in the restaurant. It had been decked out with massive bouquets of flowers and exotic plants. The guests were in full bacchanalian mode. She watched from afar until a middle-aged man with wiry glasses beckoned to her.

'Come, come, join,' he was babbling, but in her swimming suit and towel she felt and looked incongruous.

'No, no, thanks. Or maybe later. I have to change my clothes.'

'Yes, you change, you change, then come, you will enjoy, very good food, very nice.'

Katherine withdrew and rushed up to her room, opening the door carefully. Katja was awake and was nibbling on some sun-dried tomatoes and the air was filled with the scent of rose oil.

'I was reading *Mysteries of the Cosmos*. Do you realise that if you fell into a black hole you would dissolve into molecules?'

'Come on, sleepyhead, we're going to party. Downstairs. Let's get grooving.'

'Really? Must we?'

'Just for a bit. Time for a bit of hedonism. Maybe we can meet a couple of nice boys.'

'Not for me, no meat, no coffee, no alcohol, and no pricks.'

'You old maid. Get your skates on. This is going to be fun. I won't take no for an answer.'

'Must we?'

'We must dance the dance of life.'

They started dressing and, despite her initial protestations, Katja grew quite enthusiastic and she slapped on a layer of lipstick and eyeliner and soon they were ready.

By the time they arrived the party had become more heated and raucous and they noticed a few English people, conspicuous on account of their pinky white skin and sunburnt arms. They were tucked away in a corner, drinking bottles of beer. Then the man with the wiry glasses spotted the sisters and trotted over.

'Oh, I am so happy you decide to come. Very very nice. I am excited. May I ask please your good names?'

As they told him they couldn't help giggling.

'And are you enjoying Sri Lanka?'

They said they were, very much.

'Sri Lankans very good people, very good cricket players. You are playing cricket?'

They told him they didn't.

'That is pity, but you can still learn to play. I teach you some words. You know leg before wicket is when the ball is hitting the leg, umpire is the judgement, stumps are the wood, cover drive is when the ball is hit hard, googly is funny ball, England used to have great team, now is not the same, I have been in England, many times, brother-in-law have pet shop in Guilyford, I like English people, I not like football, football not gentleman game, cricket gentleman game, English tea good, but English food bad, you like Sri Lanka food? Very good curry here in hotel, hoppers good for breakfast, but maybe you are eating rice and curry also for lunch, but here not cleaning, food is good but sometimes not cleaning, I like beef curry, pancake with coconut and banana juice, you know my friend Chana, very good cook, at Seagreen View guesthouse in Galle? Sri Lankan have very very strong stomach, we can eat even petrol, we not mind, but tourist have to be careful, tourist have problem with food. Chana is at Galle. In the fort, you must go, beautiful Dutch fort, they have ayurvedic centres there, you have good massage, good for head, for mind, for body, they give good massage for body, afterwards very relax, my sister give good massage, you want that I make appointment, is not expensive, she has room near hotel, she make very nice massage, seven thousand rupees, is good price? You want go tomorrow? I take you, I have my own car, air condition, very nice.'

Katherine was laughing uncontrollably and Katja was smiling, grinning at their companion's rather disconnected monologue. Katja noticed a thickset man speaking heatedly with another, squat, burlish fellow, next to the dance floor. Behind them a few couples were dancing distractedly.

'My wife is train in India, in Kerala, she train massage in school in Trivandrum. They have good ashrams there, but she not study ashram, she prefer to make own experience, but when tsunami come she lose her shop, everything, she lose everything, you want I take you to see the Blowhole, or the stone temple, or we can go to the turtle watching, is near here we go on the beach to watch turtles, is very nice?'

The thickset man was getting angrier and more agitated and he pushed the squat fellow once or twice, shoving him near his left shoulder blade. The squat man winced and started speaking very rapidly and volubly and a few people nearby turned and watched with some concern.

'Turtles are shy though, they not always come out at night, and when we go, we must be very very quiet because they get scared. We sit on beach, like tonight, good night for turtles, we sit and wait for the turtles, sometimes they come, sometimes they don't. My name Kellum.'

The thickset man shoved the squat man again and the two girls watched as the squat man emptied his pockets and gave him some money, not much it seemed, and Katja could see that he was perspiring and looked scared. Clearly the thickset man was demanding the settlement of some debt. Then the thickset man glanced across to other men in suits, who until now had been on standby, and they strode over menacingly. At this the squat man's eyes tightened visibly. The other men waited and watched, their bodies were taut, and Katherine suddenly recognised one of them as the man from the pool. One of the men from the English party walked over to see what was happening – he placed himself between the squat man and the thickset man and it was obvious that he was trying to deflect the tension between them. The squat man was speaking very rapidly and his legs were trembling. By contrast the Englishman appeared calm, impassive. Even Kellum had picked up on the ensuing silence and unrest and had finally stopped talking and turned around in alarm. A svelte woman in a red dress hurried over to the Englishman and was telling him not to get involved. She grabbed his hand and tried to pull him away, but the Englishman seemed to want to teach the thickset man a lesson. Katherine whispered to Katja, 'I think this is probably the moment for us to leave.'

But Katja didn't reply, she was strangely compelled by the theatricality of the spectacle. The Englishman placed out his hand and pressed it firmly against the thickset man's chest. The woman in red was pleading with the Englishman now. The Englishman continued to exert pressure against the thickset man's chest, forcing him to withdraw a foot or two, but as he did so something white flashed and the Englishman instinctively clutched his side. It was bathed in blood.

And then the blood was everywhere.

The other men moved forward and formed a circle around their boss so that no one could intervene. The Englishman had started to crumple and his girlfriend was shrieking as though she was being subjected to intense physical pain. The music ceased abruptly. There was the sound of crockery and glass shattering. The thickset man turned to his lackeys and spoke rapidly. One of them grabbed a wine bottle, smashed it against a table, and gashed the woman's face with its jagged edge. People tried to intervene, but the men brandished guns and waved them in their terrified faces. The Englishman was on the floor, trying to crawl away, but the thickset man pulled out his own revolver and shot him twice in his chest and his body convulsed violently as the bullets tore into him. Then one of the men ripped off the girl's clothes and started raping her as his companions stood there without the slightest flicker of emotion or feeling. She was bleeding from the head, but he just went on thrusting into her, out of control, like some crazed ape, plugged into some newly-created circuitry of annihilation. Then he forced her down onto the dance floor and carried on, her poor naked body twitching under his bulk, her hair knotted in congealed blood. The crowd was frantic, fleeing, running for the door, screaming, shouting angry cries in Sinhala and calling for help. Katherine and Katja had turned ghastly pale. They were caught between the desire to help the woman, and the instinct for self-preservation, but finally Katherine came to some kind of resolution, realising that, as foreign women there, they would be next on these sadists' list, so she roused herself out of her stupor, frantically pulled Katja to her feet – she was on the point of collapse – and forced her to walk, dragging her away, like a swimmer who, herself half drowned, tries to guide her even more stricken companion to shore. They staggered out, not daring to look back.

Katherine struggled for a moment with the room keys. Once inside, Katja darted towards the bathroom, dropped to her knees, and vomited into the toilet, mucus and saliva dripping from her. She knelt there, trying to steady herself, heaving and sobbing. Katherine grabbed some toilet roll and wiped her sister's mouth. A minute passed and a faint tinge of colour returned to Katja's cheeks. Katherine reached for a small towel and ran cold water all over it, squeezed it, and mopped her sister's brow. Her eyes were drained and her pupils dilated and terror still wrenched her face and soul into disfigured shapes. Katherine felt weak and scared and dazed, but she forced herself to keep things together and she pressed her teeth violently to stop herself from crying and she grabbed a bottle of water, extracting it from her rucksack, and flooded a glass with it and very tenderly held out the glass to her sister's lips and Katja sipped at the water and it felt good against her parched lips and she managed to a faint smile and then she said, in a small, very frightened voice, ' . . . thank you.'

Leaving Katya there for a moment – she knew she would be all right if she could rest quietly for twenty minutes, but she knew that they didn't have twenty minutes – Katherine darted into the bedroom and began stuffing all their clothes into the rucksacks. She grabbed a small plastic bag and dumped all their toiletries inside it as Katja looked up and gaped, in awe of her sister's strength and composure.

'What's . . . what's going on?' Katja whispered.

'We're hitching a ride with the wind. We're leaving. I'm not ready to get in the wooden box yet. Those bastards are capable of anything. And there's no way we're going to sit around and wait for Sri Lankan cops to interrogate us for three days straight, which is what they would do, so let's get out now and find ourselves some shack far away from this Hellotel. Katja, darling, you have to get up, we have to leave now. Come on.'

Katherine helped her sister to her feet and steadied her. She made her drink more water and then helped her to the balcony, kicking open the door and praying the breeze and air would revive her. Katja collapsed onto the threshold between the room and the terrace. 'I can't. I'm too . . . weak . . . '

'Listen to me. The longer we stay here, the deeper shit we'll be in. We have to get out of here. You just have to get through the next forty minutes then, I promise you, I'll find you a bed and I'll put you in it and you can rest as long as you like. But now you have to be strong and brave and we have to go. Now.'

Katja listened to her sister and took it all in. She knew that she was right, of course. They couldn't stay, their lives were in danger. Who knew what was going on outside? Were the murderers now executing the other guests? Had they surrounded the hotel? Were they preventing the other guests from leaving? She had never dreamed, until then, that human beings could be so diabolical.

Katherine swung both her own and her sister's rucksacks over her back and staggered a little under the weight of them until she found her balance. She commanded Katja to take more water. Katja stared at Katherine, overwhelmed suddenly by her sister's love. She was looking at an extremely beautiful young woman whose face was filled with the world's resilience and mystery, and as she looked it was almost as though Katja was seeing her sister for the first time and at once she drew back in fear at the thought of this woman being hurt in any way or of her life being endangered and the thought gave her strength and she dragged herself to her feet.

The deserted reception area was a series of trajectories of blood and smashed glass. They could hear a babble of voices in the distance but none of the mob seemed present. They moved quickly towards the exit and were on the point of reaching the steps outside when a gruff voice barked, 'Where are you going? Come back. My gun is aimed at you.' They froze, horror rising and lashing out like a demented sea, and turned around slowly. It was the man from the pool, the one who had been watching Katherine and she felt a violent rush of nausea. With a frantic effort of will she stemmed its tide and reached out to grab Katja's hand and squeezed it tightly. They both stood there paralysed and petrified. Katherine looked into his eyes, but she could see nothing there, no light, no pity, not even anger, just two black cavities. She closed her eyes tightly and wished it would be soon over. Shadows and inchoate memories flooded up in a pre-natal blur. Time had always been unending and colossal, but now they found themselves squeezed into its final, airless chamber.

This is it this is the moment of our deaths.

Who would have thought it would end here in this hotel in Sri Lanka we won't even have time to say goodbye to each other we won't even have time to call our mum it'll all happen in a moment in the blink of an eye and we'll cease to be, cease to be anything at all we'll be a couple of dead bodies found at a scene of carnage and the English papers will say things like two young unidentified tourists were among the dead and we'll exit this world never having learnt why we were put on it and we'll depart this world like two dim-witted fools who wasted their lives and never knew how to live until now when it's too late and time has run out just when we so badly want to live and we'll never see another sunset or tree or or

Another man marched up to the first man and spoke unintelligibly and volubly in Sinhala for several moments. He seemed to be berating the first man and then slapped him with extraordinary violence on the cheek. The first man was so flabbergasted that he just stood there like some kind of dumb animal, but then, emerging from his shock, he struck the other with grinding force in the stomach and the latter instantly keeled over like a ninepin. The girls simply gaped, unable to react or move until finally Katherine, flooded by a kind of reserve energy, stirred and pulled her sister and herself out of there and it felt as though they were both clawing along the narrow space under a train, scrambling over the tracks, beneath the train's under belly, to reach freedom on the other side and as they emerged outside they broke into a run, and then ran with all their might, never thinking that their legs could carry them so swiftly down the pathway to the main road and they kept on running into the night, feeling the electric adrenaline rush of life, the exhilaration of knowing they had cheated death and had walked a tightrope spun from terror and horror, but now that walk was over and they no longer had to tread the tightrope, and contemplate the sickening abyss below, and they just kept on running, a sound of screeching trains in their ears, the brakes slammed on tight, the wheels howling and squealing and smoking as the great freight train comes to a halt just in time to avoid killing the heroine tied to the rail tracks and she is spared just as they were spared and they looked back, their heads darting in terror to catch sight of the murderers giving chase, but they weren't giving chase, and they were very nearly dead by now with the effort of this marathon in the middle of the night, but they finally stopped when they thought it was safe to do so, at a distance, a long distance from the hotel, beside the main road where the traffic passed by as it always did and the cars passed by as they always did and the wind from the cars blew as it always did and then they saw a little tuk-tuk approaching and they both yelled and danced and leapt in the air and it pulled over and they both bundled in and the driver looked at them in astonishment and Katherine ordered, 'Take us away, away from here, we don't care what the price is, just drive, quickly. Now. Now!' and he did as he was told, not daring to say a word and they saw on the back seat, next to them, a ridiculously small frying pan and on the floor next to the back seat was a large sword fish and at the sight of this they both burst into peals of laughter and they both felt that the fish and the frying pan were hilarious, wonderful, beautiful signs of life, of the life that had almost been snatched away from them and they said to the driver, 'We like your fish, it is very funny, it is very nice to see a fish,' and the driver, his surprise having now dissolved, joined in their laughter and anyone who might have seen this little party of people would have assumed they were either drunk or mad.

Eventually the laughter subsided and the girls looked at each other, dizzying currents of emotion scooting underneath, above, to the sides of them, snatches of which they spasmodically half caught, like fishermen struggling with fish too large to be brought to the water's surface, as they pulled on the line the fish fought free of the hooks, slipping into the depths, where things dwelled that could not be named. Katherine asked the driver if he knew of any hotels where they might stay the night, but the driver was unsure as this was Christmas and all the hotels were probably full. Katherine turned to assess the state of her sister's resilience and, to her surprise, found that their second encounter with death had apparently been less traumatic than the first, and that she appeared to be more buoyant and energised than ever.

'Katja . . . how are you feeling?'

'I'm alive, that's all that matters. I'm alive, I'm with you, my darling darling sister, here, in this tuk-tuk, with the warm wind in my face, the warm night, with the thought of tomorrow, sunlight, the spices of spice shops, eating seer fish on the beach, coconut pancakes, hot baths, it's all here again, we're back, we're here.' She started sobbing softly and Katherine cradled her in her arms. The driver was seriously alarmed.

'What is wrong? She ill? What I do? I stop? She need doctor?'

'No, no, she'll be fine, just take us to nearest hotel. Please.'

'Where we go? Ganesh Garden? Mango Grove? Capahanas Beach?'

'Anywhere. Just anywhere near here.'

'Is twenty-five minutes still madam.'

'That's ok.'

And now silence descended on the little group as the vehicle pushed on into the night, and daylight remained stubbornly unimaginable. It was Christmas Day, but Christmas had never seemed so abstract. They came to the first hotel the driver could find, but it was fully booked and so were the next three. Eventually Katherine, who took matters in hand while Katja dozed in the tuk-tuk, spoke with a tall Sri Lankan and practically begged him to help them – though she was aware as she did so of the possibility of her vulnerability being exploited, but she was too exhausted to remember to put on the habitual armour she wore when dealing with men. But luckily he didn't have any hostile agendas. He made a couple of phone calls and finally suggested that they try the Pastissade guesthouse on Marakollia beach. There they might find a bed for the night.

So they set off on their increasingly desperate search and the driver had to stop at a petrol station to stock up on fuel. As he did so Katherine watched her sister who was by now fast asleep. The driver puffed on a cigarette and asked Katherine if she wanted a smoke and she gratefully accepted. As she smoked the events of the night flashed through her addled mind and they were at the same time more real and more unreal than ever. She couldn't account for this and gave up trying to and just wished that the images of horror would get deleted from her brain.

When they arrived at the guest house there was at first hardly anything to suggest that it was actually a guest house. Eventually a very spindly, young man materialised and the driver spoke with him for a few conspiratorial moments, alerting Katherine's suspicions. The night was impenetrably dark but a small, bluish light burnt above the entrance. As Katja slept, Katherine tried to gauge the safety of the place – all around there was nothing but shrub and immense, gnarled trees. Two adjoining bungalows compromised the most isolated guesthouse in Sri Lanka, as far as she could ascertain – the perfect target for any more homicidal maniacs who might be roaming. The driver informed her that one of the bungalows was free, so she agreed, having no choice, and paid the driver. Very gently she woke Katja. They were both sorry to see him go. The small bellboy grew a little more friendly in Katherine's eyes as they agreed to terms and Katherine scanned him up and down – he didn't seem to present any threat. He was so slight and delicate that he made Katherine think of a stick insect. The girls dragged their luggage and themselves into the bungalow, where blue mosquito nets and a couple of beds awaited them. Katja instantly crawled into bed and said, her voice cracking with sleep's weight, 'You saved us. You were so strong, I never realised you could be so strong.'

'I didn't save us, I almost got us killed. We would have been better off staying in our room. As it was I almost got us killed. I fucked up big time.'

'No, you didn't. You got us out of there. I wanted to leave, we couldn't have stayed. It would have been insane to stay. Don't feel bad, you did the right thing.'

Katherine surveyed the bungalow and checked all the windows and locks and made sure they all fastened tightly. She splashed cold water all over her face and then urinated for an eternity. She peered at herself in the cracked mirror and had the impression that the night had aged her by years.

'Don't you think it was strange, the way that second man intervened? I really thought it was the end,' she said on her return.

'So did I.'

'How do you explain it? Divine intervention? Why were we spared?'

'I don't know. I'm too tired to understand. Too tired to speak. Just glad that we both . . . that we're both still alive. That you're with me.'

'Who were those guys? What did they want? What was wrong with them?'

'Katherine, let's talk about it in the morning. Let's sleep now.'

'They must have been the local Mafioso. They . . . oh God, it was awful . . . so awful.' Her eyes welled up with tears and she turned away so that Katja couldn't see her. For the first time that evening she allowed herself to be weak. She pulled out her cigarettes and smoked feverishly for a minute or two. Then she carried out another rigorous inspection of the bungalow and the windows and the door and the locks and watched Katja; she was in a deep sleep, and nothing about her appearance suggested the ordeal she had just been through.

Fear rose up like a long dark ribbon and wrapped itself around Katherine as she climbed into bed, wishing the night would pass quickly; but she knew that it wouldn't, that a night of insomnia awaited her. The night's images were replayed over again, the horror and relief, and unremitting intensity, until they gradually slowed.

There I was, trying to open the lid on the big black steaming soup of the unknowable, simmering away like an old witch's brew and then it seems to come open a bit and the answers, the broth, the brew, it's pouring out and it doesn't taste so bad and it isn't so black and then some fucker comes along and kicks it over and there's no time to do anything to sweep it up or mop it up or put the lid back on or anything and so it just spills everywhere and evaporates and that's the end of that and we'll never know what it was, we'll never know what it meant, just a great big bowl of nothing. So those evil cunts who almost killed us down gunned us down in cold blood who are they what are they are they just animals? No because animals are better that they are and animals are better than they are. They – I suppose they are just accidents, abortions that are alive. They go out into the big bad world and make it worse and make the badness concentrated in a small place and they gnash their teeth and make pain their credo and they have no heart or soul and not only do they have no heart or soul but they do not even know about the existence of a heart or soul and if you tried to explain the existence of a heart or soul to them they wouldn't understand it if you explained for fourteen million years they wouldn't understand. So do they, does their presence confirm that the universe is this harsh dead cold landscape no law no karma no nothing are we pieces of cosmic seaweed floating through the cold cosmos? Or does our presence have sense are we connected to the stars the exploding supernovae? Yes I know the physicists, and *Mysteries of the Cosmos* tells us we come from the stars and that the stars are in us but what does that mean what comfort is that to the dead man at Jetwing or to the raped woman at Jetwing. Why doesn't the universe help us? Why doesn't it intervene and flex some muscles? Why doesn't God get off his divine backside and stop bad things happening all the time? And why were we spared? Were we just lucky? And is luck really just the co-incidence of two or three things coming together to create a favourable outcome for the person who is then deemed to be lucky? Or does luck have its roots in something else? Something existentially meaningful? And will Kat and I now be traumatised for the rest of our lives and how can we shake off this shadow this sickness and even though the fifteen minutes after we escaped were the most alive of my life can I now enjoy the simple things like I used to without always looking around and watching my back like I am watching my back now and have I lost something tonight lost it for good and can never get it back? We are this marvellous synthesis but not a synthesis of design, a synthesis of accident and in order to know who created us we only have to look up and watch the stars with our big telescopes but that is all and we are like furniture that dust clings to that dust clings to and information clings to us and we alter and change and evolve and the very fact of our existence is the explanation for our existence so we exist because we exist and existence has begot existence and the stars that are born the billions upon billions of stars that are uncountable and are more innumerable than all the words ever spoken by all human beings who ever lived like the man says, those stars are the fabric of my being the make up of my texture my matter my form and all that we see is the cosmic dust emerging around us just as the dust emerges on a piece of furniture if you leave it long enough and intelligence and thought and self-awareness are the eventually created dust, but we like to think that with mere dust we can civilise the world and man and people but dust is dust after all and we are dust after all and where is the dialogue between us and space, us and God and us and the cosmos and where is the link? Where is the transmission, the receiver? Where is the bridge? The cosmic cable?

Where?

She fell into a fitful sleep, then woke suddenly, peering round, shining her torch into the four corners of the room. The windows had not been disturbed. The door was tightly shut and barred. She looked at Katja sleeping in a gentle cocoon and felt an infinite tenderness. She climbed back into bed and gradually the demons of the night stilled and some kind of peace was born. The little bungalow was like a lonely shuttle on a journey through space, flitting in and out of dimensions that had no beginning or end, no boundaries and the universe fluttered wildly around this fragile centre and the distilled light of day prised open the corners and angles of the room and the shadows diminished and faded and fled.

Neither intruders nor murderers had come. The day was beginning in tireless re-invention.

They ventured out and took a walk along a savagely beautiful stretch of beach that was now unveiled, having hitherto been cloaked by the night. It was as though they had been standing next to diamonds that, concealed in the darkness, they had taken for ashes. The fishermen were already out on their boats. Along the horizon a line of seven or eight slowly moving catamarans were visible, magically in harmony with the sea's motion. Their sails were bulging with the wind so that they resembled distended, pregnant bellies.

3

'How are you feeling? Katja? Could you sleep?'

'I slept like a log.'

'You weren't scared?'

'I was too exhausted to be scared.'

'I didn't sleep a wink. Or maybe I did. It's good to be crashing up against the tides. I feel . . . I don't know, what a night.'

'Let's not talk about it. Let's put it behind us. The important thing is that we're alive.'

Katherine nodded and looked earnestly into her sister's eyes. The day was starting to harden and take form, its percolating uncertainties on the point of evaporation. Katherine stared hard at the water and Katja also looked out to sea and for a moment their faces attained an uncanny similarity, almost as if both their profiles were two marginally different images of the same person. The water was glowing with sun-speckled iridescence, the wind tore through everything and at its touch all stirred with dazzling life. As Katherine stared into the sea, she no longer searched for tell-tale signs of the return of the tsunami.

Katja spoke in a very soft and even voice.

'You know . . . I was thinking . . . maybe we were spared for a reason after all. Maybe it wasn't just an accident. Maybe there was something behind it. Maybe we have something that we have to do. I don't know what. But I've learnt something. I think. To be less spoilt, to be more grateful. To try and be alive, not to take it for granted. Life. To really try and reach out and grasp it.'

'That's amazing. Diamond-brilliant. So you're cured?'

'Cured?'

'Of fear? Of unhappiness?'

'I don't know about that . . . I'm not cured. I'm just . . . I'm just able to see. Maybe I've been sleepwalking all this time. And now I've woken up at last.'

'That's amazing. Do you feel happy?'

Katja said nothing for a very long time and then turned slowly to face her sister.

'Maybe . . . maybe to be alive . . . is to be happy.'

Katherine stared at her in amazement, as though stunned by this idea. She had never imagined that such a kind of change could have been wrought in her sister, literally overnight.

'Let's not waste any more time Katherine. Let's just live. Ok? Promise?'

'But what does that mean?'

'It means . . . to start with . . . let's go back and get some Sri Lankan breakfast and some coffee and some papayas. Coming?'

Katherine nodded.

'Just give me a few moments. I need to digest. Take it all in. Wow, you're like a different person. I . . . you're so focused. You're like a laser beam. I feel . . . I feel like a screwdriver.'

'Don't be silly. You're totally and utterly amazing. You're diamond-brilliant. You're even laser-brilliant. Don't be long or I'll start to worry about you.'

Katja began to walk back to the bungalow and Katherine watched her nonchalant saunter along the sand. She watched her until she vanished inside their little bungalow, which seemed then like some kind of sanctuary or shrine. Maybe within, Katherine fondly imagined, a hidden Buddha lay sleeping, arriving at the end of his great, titanic journey, finally having managed to conquer desire, to still the raging tides of human suffering. Did he hover, like some displaced spirit, over the world, from time to time introducing some secret antidote, some benign alkaline to neutralise the acid, to still the pain. She looked out to sea, ever and again searching for the affirmation of her conjectures. She watched the configurations of clouds, their gossamer complexity dissolving into nothingness, a place unmarked on any map or chart. She stared hard into the heavens, and its corrugated, ethereal textures.

If it's true that we came from you, if it's true that the atoms that comprise life, comprise us, people, are also the same as the atoms that make up the stars, that made up the stars . . . . as that book I'm reading keeps saying. If that's true the blueprint of the universe is in me, I am the blueprint, my atoms came from those stars, I am connected and so I have nothing to fear, in a sense. In a sense.

She stared harder than she had ever stared at anything in her life, intuiting something, seeing something, maybe it was a shadow, a silhouette flickering on a cave, or maybe it was her mirror, or maybe it was a blessing or a voice or a calling or a love. She began to realise – her mind moving slowly but with ever growing confidence through a landscape of ciphers and enigmas that were no longer ciphers or enigmas but transparencies, simplicities, her mind moving through that space with no name – that if creation could design such a staggeringly complex world, could dream up and execute such infinite complexity and hold it all in such miraculous, perfectly functioning equilibrium should not such a force also be able to untie the infinitesimal (by contrast) knots in her own life, unravel the tiny entanglements of her own existence? If creation, existence, consciousness, nature, the elements, the mind of God, the cosmos, energy, call it what you will, had programmed itself into being and had then co-ordinated all the factors that allowed life to come into being and to be sustained, then did it not make sense to believe that that very same force could also dip in and out of the quagmires of our own lives and nightmares, could move a healing hand through the chaos, the pain, the problems, the traumas? In that ultimate glimpse of the ever-changing clouds, the ever-changing sea, she saw finally that there lay there the raw materials of her own salvation, her connectedness to the world, to the cosmos.

It was no longer the Buddhist driver, the wedding party, her sister, that bound her to life. It was no longer the murderers, the guns, the violence that bound her to death. A fortifying elixir was secreted into her brain. And she perceived in a grateful moment that she had been snatched perhaps from a life of perpetual questioning and wandering, there on that beach, on that arrival or departure point that the night had propelled them towards, two young women, stumbling, uncertain, but touched by beauty and, finally, by grace.

# ACKNOWLEDGEMENTS

I WOULD LIKE to thank Margarete because her gentle insistence helped me to start writing again, after such a long hiatus, Andrea Sirotti because he believed in me, Lauren Grosskopf because she went all out for me in America, Robert Karmon because his advice and support were invaluable, Jonathan Coe for his extremely generous introduction to the Italian edition of these stories, Dennis Harrison because he is an unfailing champion of my writing, and Andrew Kidd because he was incredibly generous in terms of giving me his time and literary advice. I would like to thank Dr. Patrick Burke for being such a wonderful and loyal friend – O my chevalier! I would also like to thank Alex Argus for believing that these stories possessed some merit very early on in their life. I would like to thank Nick Vecchi for his peerless friendship, his deep sincerity, and for his vintage wisdom. And finally I would like to thank my dear mother Ayko, who recently passed away. Any creativity that I have I owe completely to you, mum. This book is dedicated to your memory with love.

And finally, last but not least, I would like to thank everyone at Salt for working so hard for this book.

# NOTES

'The Meltdown' was first published in *World Literature Today*.

'The Rich and the Slaughtered' was first published in the online journal *Voyages*.

'Island' first appeared in the Oxford-based anthology *The Sandspout*.

This book has been typeset by SALT PUBLISHING
LIMITED using Neacademia, a font designed by Sergei
Egorov for the Rosetta Type Foundry in the Czech
Republic. It is manufactured using Creamy 70gsm, a
Forest Stewardship Council™ certified paper from Stora
Enso's Anjala Mill in Finland. It was printed and bound
by Clays Limited in Bungay, Suffolk, Great Britain.

LONDON
GREAT BRITAIN
MMXIX